W9-AHF-917

Autumn of the Royal Tar

From my days up in Maine —

[illegible]

BRUCE STONE

Autumn of the Royal Tar

A LAURA GERINGER BOOK

AN IMPRINT OF HARPERCOLLINS*PUBLISHERS*

Autumn of the Royal Tar

 Printed in the United States of America.
For information address HarperCollins Children's Books, a division of HarperCollins Publishers, 10 East 53rd Street, New York, NY 10022.

Library of Congress Cataloging-in-Publication Data
Stone, Bruce.
Autumn of the Royal Tar / Bruce Stone.
p. cm.
Summary: When a ship sinks off the coast of Maine, twelve-year-old Nora tries to help the survivors, who include an orphaned boy and an elephant.
ISBN 0-06-021492-9. — ISBN 0-06-021493-7 (lib. bdg.)
[1. Shipwrecks—Fiction. 2. Island—Fiction. 3. Maine—Fiction.] I. Title.
PZ7.S875945Au 1995 95-6122
[Fic]—dc20 CIP
AC

Typography by Al Cetta
1 2 3 4 5 6 7 8 9 10
❖
First Edition

for Dorothy

Autumn of the Royal Tar

ONE

"Is he three weeks out yet?" I asked Mama.

"Three weeks to the day," she answered. She took hold of the barrel by its rim and rolled it farther down the bank, into the sun. It was October, late Saturday. Mama wanted to work in the sun. She wanted to be warm and she wanted to work outside. Father would be sailing home.

Mama held the barrel tilted against the sloping bank. She nudged a flat stone under with her toe. She let go the barrel too fast and the brine lapped over the rim.

"Oh bless it, now look at this." She jumped back and held her skirt out toward me. She wrung it with both hands and let it fall. The stain reached from the hem to her knees, like a wrinkled cloud full of rain.

"It's just my old Boston dress," Mama said. "My last Boston dress, but then it's been a long time since Boston."

"A year more than me, right, Mama?"

"A year more than you, Nora, that's right. Nearly fourteen come the spring." Mama sighed and smoothed her skirt. "Fourteen years on this rock in the ocean."

Mama needed cheering.

"Tell me how it was when you were a girl," I urged her. "Tell about the Boston streets and the shops and the sailors with brass buttons. And especially the part about Sunday."

"You know it all, even the Sunday." Mama tried to laugh.

"Please, Mama," I begged.

She wrung the wet skirt in her hands once more. "Some other time perhaps, Nora." She turned to look across the water.

"Then I will tell it," I insisted. "You lived on Captain Street . . ."

"Captains' Row," she corrected.

"Yes, you lived on Captains' Row . . ."

"All right. We lived on Captains' Row, straight brick houses taller than barns with glass in all the windows and some with three panes bowing out to look both ways up and down the streets. We could watch, from the second floor, the carriages passing back and forth, the men strolling arm in arm down to the wharf to see the Sunday trade, smoke from their pipes trailing behind like fine ribbon. Then later, downstairs in the parlor, we would arrange the chairs to sit our guests in circles and the uncles would tell about the South Seas or Jamaica. Then finally the children would recite their verses and the kitchen would fill with steam from puddings and sweetmeats. Of course, whichever of us recited best and longest was named to bless the pudding."

"And were you ever named, Mama?" I asked.

"I suppose I was," Mama said.

"You said almost every Sunday. Oh Mama, tell it right."

"I was named many times, yes, certainly more than once, I recall."

"And tell about the dresses now. Did you wear brocade and velvet trimmed with lace?"

"That's enough for now. Boston is a world away." Mama dropped the damp hem and rubbed her hands together. She held them, palms up, against her face and wrinkled her nose.

"Don't you smell sweet now, Mama," I told her.

"And so don't you, my Nora," she said. "Now let's get these last ones made. My Boston stories will keep better than the fish."

We were making fish, salt cod. I cleared the hard dried ones off the cedar flake and stacked them along a plank against the house. When I got back to the flake, Mama unbuttoned her sleeves, plunged her hands into the barrel, and handed me two split fish, each piece big as a shingle.

"Here. Start these in the middle, Nora," Mama ordered. I laid the fish out, silver sides down, across the flake. Its latticed strips of cedar darkened with the brine.

Mama stood at the barrel, her back to me. She stared off down the Thorofare, where Father's cutter, *Veto,* would appcar. Its sails would rise like white wings from the western shore. They could block the sun before it even reached the Camden Hills.

"Three weeks is twenty-one days," I called toward Mama's back. A wind ruffled the water and flattened waves as it moved ashore.

Mama spun and hugged herself around the waist. "Now stop your counting. Stay busy and let's finish. Your father has to keep the ocean's time, you should know by now."

"I do, Mama," I said. "But you count too. You make X's on your calendar every day he's out."

"I make crosses, Nora, not X's. And it isn't counting like you do. I just like to mark the days."

Crosses, not X's. Marking, not counting. Mama certainly had her distinctions.

Finally, the flake was most near filled with fish. Then from up near the house came a scratching and a clatter. The hard stacked fish spilled from the plank. Mama ran toward the house. I watched Bob and Spindle fleeing for their lives.

"Shoo, get, bold thieving cats," Mama hooted after them. She chased them, snapping her skirt like a whip. They scuttled around my feet and headed for the barrel, Mama right behind. "Sneaky, cunning orphan cats," she hissed.

She saw them hide behind the barrel and brushed past me. "Hush now," she whispered, but I was saying not one word already.

Mama tiptoed up, squatting just this side the barrel. She took it by the rim, tight in her hands. She looked at me and nodded. Then she bucked up, off her haunches, still with her hands clamped onto the barrel. Straight over on top of the cats she tips it and brine gushes in a huge green wave, catching the cats as they scattered, washing down the bank and over the edge like a riptide.

"Look out! Barrel! Barrel!" I hollered—a stupid way to warn a cat. But I watched the barrel catch the slope. It rolled on its side, then spun over the edge to where the cats disappeared down the bank. I heard it crack hollow and wooden. When I reached the shore, its staves lay scattered like jackstraws just above the tide.

TWO

I picked my way along the shore, stepping among the slickened stones and ooze. I tried to figure how many times I'd had to save old Bob and Spindle. Weekly, sometimes every day it seemed, when Mama's ire got provoked. Father had saved them first, of course, over to Castine. Some boy was set to pitch them overboard tied up in a sack. Father brought them home instead, for Owen, three summers gone. I was nine and Owen six. That's as old as Owen got to be. He had them, both the cats, barely a fortnight before the fever turned for good. After Owen, Mama called them orphan cats. Mama shut them from the house, so Father put them in the barn. I tried to watch them some, but Mama wished they'd disappear. It had to do with Owen, I suppose.

It got so bad. Father was gone two months after that. I remember because of Owen's stone. It says July 3, 1832. Father sailed two days after and got home for my birthday, September 5. That's the longest he'd ever been out one stretch. Sixty-two days. One day short of nine weeks. That's when I started counting.

"Hey, Bob, hey, Spindle!" I shouted, tripping along the water's edge. I tangled a foot in sea grape and tumbled to my knees. They stung when I stood again, and I bent to wipe the mud away.

I headed eastward where the shoreline curved back into a small mudflat. There stood Mama in the shadow of our chimney where it bends over the bank late of an afternoon. She balanced at the edge, arms waving, and called out over the wind: "Down here, Nora. Safe and sound. Unfortunately."

I found them, sure enough, nesting in a bed of kelp. They were licking in a fury, curled against each other between two loaf-shaped rocks.

"Wretched creatures," I scolded, but not harshly. I plucked them free and climbed the bank. I squeezed them up beneath my arms for warmth.

"There's another dress ruined," Mama called from above.

"Barrel too," I reminded her. "All stove up for good."

"Barrels and brine just so much wood and stink," Mama said. She lifted the hem of my dress and smelled. Her face shrank. "A fine dress is a signature of elegance. Of a lady."

"Fine dress, Mama? Not this scratchy muslin thing."

Mama ignored me. She dropped the hem and walked back toward the house. I followed, Bob and Spindle still snugged tight beneath my arms. Their rough tongues ran across my fingers.

Mama stooped above the pile of tumbled cod. She

stacked it on the plank once more and started scolding. "At least we're done with making fish for this year, anyways. Let's get this downcellar. And keep those animals away—I mean it." She shook a finger at the cats. They clutched against my sides and grabbed some with their claws.

"Yes, at least we're done," I tried agreeing. "Don't forget it rained all August long, and July was thick o' fog. Too wet to make the fish."

"When finally we got good ones, yes." Mama meant the early catch was bad, all wormy. Father gave it most away to Lem Carver. Lem chopped it up for chum. A pack of gulls trailed his skiff all summer, shrieking like an angry cloud.

I ran to stow the cats back in the barn. I helped Mama carry all the cod downcellar. After, we went outside once more and stood beside the flake. "This last will have to make the best of tomorrow's sun," Mama said. "The other's done and good and should get us far along as March."

And so we had the cod to last till spring. I closed my eyes to imagine the first batch warming by the fire. Mama's savory chowder—thick and hot, potatoes, onions, cream, a clot of butter melting over top, in yellow streaks, like sunset. But thin by February, and hardly more than salt pork and flour comes the last in March. Winter takes so long.

"Now get that horrid dress off, Nora," Mama ordered. I started toward the house. But Mama hooked me by the elbow. She pulled me halfway to the barn and stood me next to the well. She unbuttoned my dress behind. I pulled it off and Mama stretched it over the side of the well. She drew a bucket and doused it good, then left it out to dry.

"Pure filth. I don't know how it's possible. I haven't seen so much mud since the Cubbyhole, the day that you and . . ." But Mama caught herself and stopped. She was remembering that day at the Cubbyhole, where me and Owen used to wade in the gray ooze. The Cubbyhole was a cove so flat we could walk the tideline out and back, taking most the afternoon and evening of a full-moon tide in August. When the sun shone full bright all day and the mud would steam like sea smoke in January. And when the water edged in, it warmed so that times I could just hitch my hemline until my skirts were wrapped around my waist and let the tide wash like a warm bath around my legs. Owen, still hardly big enough, would stoop to roll his trousers legs up around his knees. Problem was, first step anyway and his cuffs was dragging through the mud, unrolled again and dragging.

Once came a riptide. It caught Owen leaning the wrong way, and washed him full over on his backside. I dredged him out, and he coughed seawater all the way home. The ooze had dried so fast that, once home, he seemed from the back more like the dead bark of an elm, crusting over and cracking. And me hardly better for my own part, mud green and mossy like the north side of the same tree. So that it took us more than an hour of scrubbing at the wellside before Mama allowed as how we might resemble, however slightly, her "blessed, precious" children. Mama, of course, assigned me the blame. She scorned my "pitiable judgment in the matter of Owen's care"—that's how she told it to Father, almost word for word. And Father agreed if only to relieve her humor. From that day on I had certainly stained myself in Mama's eyes. And it wouldn't wash off like the mud. . . .

"May as well get a fire started inside," Mama was saying. "You can slide the tub across by yourself, yes?" I nodded that I could. It still weighed more than me, but I could at least scrape it across the floor to hearth-side.

"Shall I scrub my hair, too, Mama?" I asked.

"Scrub everything, and twice. You smell like low tide. As do I. Father's had enough of sea smells, breathing salt for three weeks. He needs to smell a lady for a while."

She turned to face the well. She lifted her skirt across its stones and splashed the pale stain where the brine had spilled. She wrung it out. Water splashed across her shoe tops.

"Now get inside. You're going to catch your . . ." But Mama couldn't finish it that way, not since Owen. ". . . a chill," she finished. She never missed a chance to remind me of catching chills, like Owen after the Cubbyhole.

She never blamed me, not in so many words. But I knew what she thought. Even later, more than a year, when Owen took the fever, she kept me away, farther and farther the worse it grew. It was for my own good, she always said, but I half thought she figured I was the contagion. So it was me who lost hold of Owen first, then all of us together later, and for good.

Suddenly Mama's hands flew to her skirt, smoothing and patting, fretting over the faded cloth. She lowered her stare to the puddle at her feet. I took the chance to turn her thoughts to me. "Mama," I began, "I wondered if I could use the other soap . . ."

"My soap?"

"The lilac, yes, please, Mother."

"Well, your father . . ."

"But you said he'd want us to smell like ladies, and I was thinking some. That rendered lye is brutal harsh . . ."

Mama lifted her face to mine and studied my eyes. "You're a bold one too, Miss Nora Beverage. You and your unholy cats." She ran a hand across her lips, like to erase any chance a smile might grow there. "I imagine you're old enough for perfumed soap. We'll see. Now get inside. And don't waste it."

"It's only soap, Mama," I answered, and ran toward the house.

"Only *my* soap, you mean," Mama called behind me. "Your father's apt to confuse us. Both smelling all of lilac, me and you, smelling the both the same!"

THREE

Before my hair had dried, Mama sent me down the street for some wicks. "If your father gets home tonight, I want to see his face by a good clean light. I know he'll want to see yours too," she had said.

The rough gentlemen were waiting. Always there. Giles Wooster spotted me first. "Good day to ye, Mistress Nora. Look, lads, it's the Cap'n's girl. Come to call." He hurried across to block my path to Staples' door. The others closed around him.

"You're a fetchin' young lady. Ain't she cunnin', boys?" I tried to push around him to the door. He put his face against mine. He smelled. His whiskers scratched like moss.

I told them all I had come to get wicks for my mother. I had to get right back, I said. Giles asked when Cap'n B. was hauling home.

"Tonight. It's been three weeks out," I told him. "To the day. We're expecting him right soon."

"He'd better make it fast, Miss Nora. This weather don't look to hold much longer."

I looked out to the Thorofare. Flat calm. The sky empty and blue. "Looks mighty clear to me, Giles Wooster," I told him. I pointed straight above us.

"Well, she might seem so," Giles answered. He looked straight up, mouth open, mostly toothless. "Clear overhead for certain, as you say, Miss. But they ain't neither me nor you that's headin' up in that direction by and by."

Well gracious, didn't they howl at that one. In old Giles Wooster's case it was probably a sorry fact. And I said so: "You're heading that way," I told him and pointed straight down between my feet. "And they might not even let you in there unless you'd know enough to take a bath."

So that cleared me the way to Staples' door at last. Mama always said never to exchange words with that bunch, but it's only so much one can endure. Mama says they don't know better, given that they never lived anywhere but on the island. And then she blames their idleness. Father calls them mudscratchers. Summers they dig clams. Winters, maybe cut some ice. Not strong enough for lumbering anymore, nor smart enough to fish. So they got nothing else but each other and simple meanness.

And they envy us Beverages and anyone else who comes from "away"—which means anyplace else in the entire world save for Cold Harbor Island. And they know my father's smart and good and skippers his own boat, and Mama dresses fine and reads and writes and has taught me much the same. Worst of all, she shuns their company like it were a contagion. And that must irritate the most.

So I went into Staples' and bought some wicks for Mama and some rock crystal sweets for myself. I would take the candy home and tell Mama it was something nice for Father.

When I left the store, the rough gentlemen were gone. I turned out onto the landing and started home. A hand clutched at my shoulder as I came just past the icehouse out in front of the store.

"I just wanted to say . . ." It was Giles. He walked beside, almost curtsying as he walked. "They's sportive lads, Miss Nora. It was just a chance to lark around some."

He was trying to apologize. "Never mind, Giles," I told him. "It's no great sin to me."

Still, his hand held tighter on my shoulder. He spun me around to face back to the store. "Look out easterly," he said. He pointed over the gray shingles of Staples' roof. "See them clouds?" Three long strands of clouds, like ragged yarn, curled high off in the eastern sky. "They come in high and thin at first. Nor'easter sky. It's early, sure. But watch and see, it'll be blowing up before dark. The boats is all out there tonight."

He nodded back toward the town float. It was empty. Everyone had moored their boats out in the middle of the Thorofare to ride out rough weather without slamming into each other. Every singular craft, dory or ketch, floated nosing into the gentle chop heading out to the Thorofare's ocean end, toward Atlantic weather.

"That's all I meant to say, miss. If Cap'n's bound for home. It's not to scare ye, miss."

I scanned the horizon, above the line of blue treetops, and across the green-gray water. Father always said a sign was birds. They knew to clear out first, to find a place before the weather broke. The sky was empty either way. Except for the cormorants—a black clump huddled on a ledge just beyond the float. Like Giles and the rest.

Giles saw me watching them. "Oh, them. They's dumb as buckles. Just get themselves to rocks and hunker down. They'll be there forever."

"I'll tell Mama, Giles. About the storm. We'll keep a watch. It'll be all right."

"That's right, Miss. Don't fret. You say a prayer for Cap'n B." He gave my shoulder a little squeeze and released it. "And maybe I'll do likewise."

I turned toward home and started down the lane. In five more steps or so, I heard his voice one final time: "I hope you caught that, Lord. Giles Wooster's gonna pray tonight." I turned to see him, head thrown back, howling at the sky. Those three strands of clouds had moved straight overhead.

FOUR

When I got home Mama was washing the glass chimneys while the lamps waited on the table. I set the wicks beside them.

"Just leave the change there beside the lamps," Mama said.

"No change. I got this here, for Father." I held the rock crystal out in my hand.

"And for who else?" Mama asked. She dried the chimneys against her apron. "Here, put these on the hearth to dry."

The chimneys crunched along their bottom rims when I set them gently on the hearthstone. I sat back at the table and Mama reappeared from her room, pulling a brush through her hair.

"Dear Nora, that's much too close." Mama moved the chimneys back from the fire. They sizzled when she set them down. The water inside them turned to steam.

"Here, pull a chair around." Mama sucked at her fingers where the chimneys had scorched them. I pulled a chair around beside the table. Mama picked up the brush and arranged herself behind me.

"Lean back," she ordered. I tilted my head back

across the chair. Mama took my hair in one hand. With the other she brushed back from my forehead.

"We'll be using this to sweep the floor, come summer." Mama yanked my hair back like it was a bell rope in the church. It touched the floor between her feet.

"Now, Mama, you promised. Not a lick until I'm thirteen. And then only if I say so." Mama had been yearning to cut my hair for so long a time. Father made her pledge no mention of it. But Mama couldn't abide his pacts, especially when he was three weeks out or more.

So Mama made two braids. She handed me the glass, to watch in. Still, I dared not say a word. She looped the braids into spirals above each ear and pinned them tight against my head.

"That will have to do you, Nora." She scraped her chair back up against the table.

"They're done right handsome, Mama," I said. "Thank you."

Mama trimmed the wicks, trying to ignore the compliment. She twisted the wicks into the lamps and left them to soak.

"Such vanity," she sniffed, and marched to the pantry.

I laid the glass on the table. Mama crossed to the fire. She pulled a splinter of wood from the kindling box and held it into the flame. "They say downstreet it's going to blow tonight."

"Do they? Who might 'they' be?" Mama carried the burning splinter over to the table and touched the flame to the lamp wicks. The lamps went *woof* and caught. Two threads of soot twisted into O's. I watched them float like black halos to the ceiling boards and disappear.

"I asked a question of you, Nora. Who talked to you downstreet?" Her face tightened against the brightness of the lamps.

"Giles Wooster was who," I answered. "They're all moored in the Thorofare. The float is empty. So's Staples' wharf."

"Giles Wooster, indeed." She turned the lamps down until the flames glowed blue and white. "The only thing Giles Wooster knows about the weather is what John Barleycorn tells him, the old fool. . . ."

I fetched the chimneys and fixed them on the lamps. Mama continued sharp, angry now. "I figure your father knows enough about the intentions of the weather to stay a day ahead of Giles Wooster. He'll be all right." Then Mama patted the table beside me. "Now clear it off. I intend to make the biscuit."

I put one lamp back on the highboy, the other by the pantry.

"Don't make the biscuit, Mama. That'll make it sure he's home tonight." Mama always said Father was sure to return early anytime she hadn't done her baking. She said it was his way of being contrary. But Mama was already flouring the table. A cloud of white powder rolled across from Mama onto me.

"I'm making the biscuit," she announced. "It can be hard as granite before your father returns, but I'm making the biscuit all the same."

So.

Mama mixed her flour and soda, and cut the lard into her crockery bowl. She snugged the bowl up under her left arm and set to beating the biscuit two hundred strokes, spoon clenched in her right fist. I stood with her, at the window. We watched the water, how it chopped and flattened under a soft wind. It grew slick and gray, a greasy slate, and darkened in the shadow of the spruce. The sun was nearly gone.

Later, as the house filled with the hot powdery smell of biscuit, we ate supper. I could barely tell the turnip from the potato from the stew meat in my bowl, the biscuit filled my senses so. When they were done, Mama allowed us each one apiece and *that was all*. I smothered mine with raspberry jam. Mama covered the rest and placed them by the fire.

After that, we cleaned. I scrubbed the table twice and swept the floor. I carted wood inside.

"That should be ample till January," Mother teased. "You'd might be getting on to bed now, Nora."

"But, Mama, it's so early still."

"No earlier than any night you go to bed. Your father is home when he's home. Tomorrow soonest, looks to me."

"But, Mama, I'll read my lessons, I'll . . ."

Mama folded her apron and pointed it toward the stairs. "I've said it once. Twice becomes a fault. I'll be right here, down here. Your lessons can wait another day."

Her arm rose stiffly at her side, the apron still pointing my way to the stairs. I walked in their direction. "I could keep a lamp in my window, upstairs, for Father, I mean. Not to read, but just in case."

"The man knows where we live, I should think." She took one step toward me and I was gone half up the stairs that fast.

"Your father hardly needs a house afire just to light his way. Now go." And I heard the apron pop like a whip at the end of her arm, and I felt more than ever like the orphan cats, shooed to oblivion in their dark cold barn.

FIVE

I changed into my gown by candlelight. The mattress crunched, the ropes sagged under as I rolled into bed. I snuffed the candle out.

Downstairs, another log settled on the fire. It crunched the ashes underneath and settled, sighing in a long shrill wheeze. Mama's rocker groaned against the floorboards. It went *reesh* on downstroke, *russh* on the way back. *Reesh-russh, reesh-russh* went the rocker, back and forth—and then between the sounds came knitting needles, chattering away in Mama's lap.

I settled back and listened to the sounds. Then, almost asleep, I started up in bed. It had grown dead quiet downstairs. Then I heard Mama's voice—but was she talking to Father, was he home at last? I strained to hear his voice deep and hollow in the room below. But only Mama, murmuring low, the words running together like a prayer, a song. And pauses filled with rattling paper in between, the tissue-thin rattle of paper, of pages, and then Mama's voice once more. She was reading her "lessons," as she called them—her scriptures.

Father couldn't get her near the church hardly

anymore. She'd hold her open Bible upside down and spread its binding over her hands like the two sides of a roof. "This is the only house of worship I will need forever more," she once proclaimed. Father knew it had come with the changes after Owen, and let her be.

Downstairs, Mama was rocking in time with the words. She had a beautiful voice, it was true. I remembered how she used to sing for Owen, her voice soft as a birthday wish, how I would sometimes sing beside her, Owen in her lap, Mama in her chair, rocking, rocking. It was Owen's lullaby, a song of Mama's making. I rolled over on my side and fell into sleep, trying hard to see Owen's white round face. But remembering only the song:

Remember me fondly,
Think something kindly,
I bid you safe passage
Across the deep sea—
And rock in my dreams
Like a ship on calm water
And let the wind bring you
Back safely to me.

I sat up suddenly in the dark and struck out to push it away . . . something, a cold thin hand at my cheek, along my neck. I felt nothing but a thread of air, a cold wind spinning in my room, only the wind after all. A gust pushed against the house, rattled at the window. I could see the flake outside now lifted up and tumbling on its side, spilling fish along the ground. Sparks pulled from the chimney flew flat across to the apple trees. They jiggled in the bare black branches, like moths on fire, and went out.

Old Giles was right. It was blowing up fierce. I said a hurried prayer for Father—and hoped Giles had kept his promise for the same. The wind seized on the house and shook it. Beads of rain flashed through the light below.

I stared off into the night and listened to the wind. It came like the ocean, in waves, harder and louder, most near a gale now. Giles had said it would be a nor'easter. They could push the water up so high it gorged into the Thorofare, and tides ran double high. It chased the fish and lobster to deeper water. They were near gone anyhow, the season over now for good until next April, when the spring crawl brought them in from colder water way offshore. The men would stay inside the winter and build their traps. And Father would be home.

It must have been dead late. I looked off east, more to hear than see where the storm was blowing from.

And then, a wonder! The sun was rising, red and orange and yellow all at once, just off Coombs' Point. But how, in the middle of the night, in the middle of a gale? I turned back into the room and closed my eyes and blinked and looked again.

But still, brighter, closer, it glowed, and I thought,

how beautiful, how wonderful a sight. But the light never rose. It flashed orange and came bigger, brighter, licking over the water. Where the water met the sky. And the ragged bottom of the low dark clouds glowed like coals with its light. And the light came closer still, floated into the Thorofare like a burning island on a tide of flames. Until the wall of spruce along the shore of Stimpson's Island caught its furious light and bounced it back along the dark-bright water. Flames, a burning on the water, a ship ablaze, adrift and burning orange and yellow. A wonderful, terrible sight.

I threw off my gown, found my stockings, my boots, pulled on my dress, raced downstairs. Thinking, Please not him, not this way, twenty-one days out and now this, horrible, horrible . . . not that . . .

Not Father.

"Mama, Mama," I called. "Fire! Off Coombs' Point. It's a ship, must be a ship." Mama stirred in her chair. The Bible fell from her lap. She grabbed the rocker's arms and tried to waken.

"I'm . . . I dozed." Her face went blank with puzzlement.

I grabbed the back of her rocker and settled my voice. "Mama, it's been storming. I was watching out the window. I saw a light down Coombs' way. I think there's something on fire out there. In the Thorofare. We should—"

Mama pushed stiffly from the rocker. "Your window," she muttered. "Your window."

I steered her to the bottom of the stairs. She went up to my room. "Fetch the lantern, Nora," she ordered, her voice trailing down the stairs.

I pulled the lantern from the chest. Mama dressed and handed me an oilskin coat, Father's. It dragged along the floor. Mama wrapped her head in a scarf and we went out to the kitchen, where she knelt by the fire and lit the lantern.

She turned away from the hearth. Her face shone pink and afraid. "You better pray it's not—"

"I have," I interrupted. "I already have."

SIX

Outside the wind tore at us hard. Father's coat flapped behind me like a sail come undone. Mama's scarf blew from her head and caught in an overhead branch. We pushed on as far as the road toward Coombs' Point and found the trail the diggers used to reach the inlet farther on. Mama held the lamp above her head in front, and me by the hand in back. We crouched and picked our way past branches, over lichen-crusted rocks, through tangles of blowdown trees and rotted trunks slick with rain.

We followed the glow hanging high and orange above the trees up ahead. We soon could smell the burning as we came closer. Finally, Mama pushed us clear through low-hanging balsam and we clambered up a rocky hillock to the shore.

"Oh." Mama caught her breath. "Lord bless us." I fell back against a rock and sat. My legs wouldn't have managed anyhow. Maybe two, three hundred yards offshore, a great fire raged and flamed. It was a side-wheel steamer, the first I'd ever seen, its railing laced with fire, its pilot house a giant spout of a torch reaching straight up in the sky. The boat seemed twice as long as our barn, longer even than the *Veto*, Father's cutter. Its big side-wheel rested with its bottom half in the water. Around its circular cover up top the steamer's name was painted black in curling letters: *Royal Tar.*

Something on board exploded. A bolt of flame shot up through the bow.

Mama reached a hand back and rested it on my head. "Look starboard, Nora. They're lowering to."

Against the flames I saw the outlines of two men swinging axes at the ropes. A jolly boat swung sideways and lurched into the water. Figures scrambled overboard, into the boat. Others jumped into the water and clung to her gunwales.

At the very center deck a lone figure stood amid the flames. He tugged a giant sail up the boat's solitary mast.

"There's a good man," Mama called. "See, he's gonna run her aground." If he could get the sail up fast enough, the wind would do the rest. The ship could blow before the wind and run aground. Near enough to jump or scramble ashore.

The figure hauled at the sail. It caught the wind and strained against its lines. A gust blew from the side and the sail luffed and slapped back against the mast. The boat swung toward shore. The figure was swallowed in the canvas, then once more the sail bellied out and pulled the steamer right at Mama and me. Other figures ran from rail to rail. I thought I could hear them calling over the wind.

"They've got her now," Mama cried. She leaned out from the rocks and swung her lantern high and arcing toward the sea.

"She's burnt, it's catching," I shouted. "Stand clear!" I shrieked into the wind, and my voice blew back into my face.

We watched how the fire ran like a snake up the lines, along the canvas. Soon the sail blazed square and white against the sky like the gates of heaven opening unto glory. But the lines burned first, and gave, and when they snapped, the sail blew clear. It curled in the wind and floated out across the water. It hung, then settled featherlike across the water where it burned and hissed and disappeared.

"Bless their souls, she's lost for good," Mama moaned. She sat beside me, lantern at her feet. I offered to run back downstreet, to cry for help.

"There's nothing . . ." Mama just shook her head. "Nothing to do, just lost." Still, I stood and took the lantern in my hand. They must know they are by land, I thought. The light at least could guide them, give them something, hope.

More figures scrambled on deck from below. The mast burned, a needle of flame. It crashed on deck, the figures scattered. More leapt overboard. The steamer rocked end to end. It could find a ledge and snap in half. Another boat, a dory, lowered from the side. Three figures, men, pushed clear and bucked along before the waves.

The sea washed up across my feet. Mama leaped from her rock. "Come, Nora, let's get back. There's nothing we can do. That anyone can do. The water's coming in."

I wanted to stay, to watch. And then somehow I felt ashamed, just to stand and watch.

Mama hooked me by the elbow and spun me around. "Step careful now, Nora," she warned. I balanced with the lantern out to the side. I turned once to look back. The steamer still rocked and burned.

"All right, Mama," I said. I stood and bent beneath the balsam branches. Yet something white—a cloud, or like a cloud—flashed in the corner of my eye. It came from back down the Thorofare, a puff of white, triangular. I pulled back, breaking free from Mama's grip. I stumbled once, then caught myself against the rocks.

"Nora, come right now," Mama warned. But I just watched the white, the small three-sided patch. It came sliding out of the darkness. Beneath it, a sleek black hull nosing, tacking against the wind. The jibsail snapped once and the boat came to. It was the *Veto*! I was sure, even before I could see, in the light cast by the fire, the brassy letters shining just beneath the bowsprit.

"Him, Mama," I called. "It's Father, in the *Veto*. He's home, this way, over here."

Mama picked her way in silence back across the rocks. She watched beside me as the cutter slid up the

Thorofare, its hull like a blade flashing the orange light of the flames.

"Thomas," Mama whispered into the storm. Then she took the lantern from my hand and held it overhead. "He's not there yet, dearest," she told me. "Will be, though, home soon. Three weeks out."

"And then some, Mama," I said. "Three weeks out and more.'"

The *Veto* passed in front of the *Royal Tar* and then swung about. It pulled up alongside the burning steamer from behind. The jibsail fluttered and dropped to the deck.

"Provide for my Thomas," Mama prayed. She dropped the lantern to the rocks and held her hands against her face to block the brilliant light. The *Veto* had been eclipsed by the blazing steamer. Only the *Veto*'s mast stood shining through the flames.

The *Royal Tar* pitched in the wind. I strained to hear against the storm and thought I heard a terrible moaning, like the sound of spirits in torment, low and hollow and forlorn.

"Mama, I think I hear—"

"I can hear it too," Mama said. She hushed and so did I and we listened. "Must be the grinding of the hulls together—I hope," Mama added.

"Must be. I hope so," I told her.

Then we stood and watched the fire in silence. It was strange how I couldn't look away. I had always been a looker into fires, drying my hair or watching the blue flames lick against the kettle bottom. Sometimes I would even put my hand out toward the flames, to see how long, how close, I could keep it there.

The *Royal Tar*'s pilot house finally gave way. It crumbled in on itself, collapsing to the deck and down, swallowed into the hold and sending up a rush of sparks.

"She's done for," Mama cried out at last. She clasped her skirt around her knees and watched the sky go dark.

Suddenly the black hull of the *Veto* slid from behind the flames. "They're clear!" I shouted. "Look, Mama, Thomas is bringing them home." Mama twisted her head to look at me, a curious stare. I confess I don't know where that "Thomas" came from. Neither did Mama, to judge by her look. "Father," I corrected, and Mama looked away.

The *Veto*'s jibsail popped out in front and the cutter moved back up the Thorofare. Mama made ready to go. I retrieved the lantern and handed it back. But still I had to watch the *Royal Tar*'s final moments. Mama seemed to understand. The steamer was hardly more than a slip of fire, a long bright scar burning in the stormy chop. It pitched once more and gave a thunderous crack, splitting not in half, but opening lengthwise like a pod. The boat sank slowly then, and grandly regal, and from inside blew a cloud of smoke so black it made the night seem pale.

And then, like a vision, from out of the smoke rose two white birds, white and big, with scythe-shaped wings and the most curious big bills sagging like empty purses beneath. They had sloopy gangly necks that pumped back and forth as their wings beat. But when they finally rose high enough, they just held their wings straight out and glided like gulls, circling and bumping in the rough winds before they disappeared.

"Did you see them, Mama?" I asked.

Mama stood beside me and shivered. "I suppose I saw them . . . saw something, Nora. Odd birds, is all."

"Like something from the ark, Mama. Maybe it's a sign, a miracle." I watched the sky to see, but they were gone.

"The ark. Well, maybe. Hardly. Not half the miracle we need," Mama said. "Let's go back now. I think we've seen enough."

SEVEN

Downstreet was a fair commotion. The landing swarmed with folks like mid-June before the Portland steamer docks. Even the Widow Parker was there, with her son Thayer right beside, still in his nightshirt, slicker over top. Giles and his gentlemen were down to the end of Dyson's Wharf, holding tight each to his own piling. Mr. Staples' store shone brighter than Christmas. The Cooper boys had somehow gotten out to the town float. They crouched and balanced on its slick boards and passed around torches while the float tilted in the waves. There was hooting and hallos and catcalls and whistles and bright lights on the water, a festive frantic scene for the shank end of an October storm.

Mama found a corner of the bait shed down this end of Dyson's Wharf. She was drenched through and so was I. We huddled together close and Mama urged my hitching over more but the eaves were sparse and the rain still flew in our faces. The water washed up between the planks and lapped across our feet. At our backs, the clapboards failed sorely in their work. A board let slip and caught Mama across the back. It hung from one nail and waggled with each gust.

Finally the *Veto* swung around out of the dark. She slid from windward and smacked broadside into the wharf. The pilings splintered and the wharf hove sideways. Down at this end, Giles pitched back on his heels. He wrapped both arms about his piling this time and slid down to his knees. From over the *Veto*'s sides some crew vaulted to the wharf. Lines flew through the air and slapped wet against planks. The lines pulled tight, and soon the *Veto* was lashed snugly to the pilings. By now the whole town seemed clustered on the shaky wharf, and edging closer to the boat, waiting. I started off to join them but Mama pulled me back.

At last Father appeared on deck. He stood at the *Veto*'s railing and bent toward the crowd. He pulled off his cap and pushed his black hair back from his forehead. Handsome as ever, he stood there just the briefest moment and puzzled over the townsfolk making such a strange homecoming. He squinted against the glare of their lanterns and seemed to ask a question. Amid murmurs and a great swell of confusion the mob spied Mama and then me. It rose to a clamor. Voices started calling out: "Mrs. Beverage, Mrs. Beverage," and some were calling "Nora."

Mama flushed. Embarrassed, she turned to me. "Howling after us like wild beasts. Imagine!"

Still they called. "Mrs. Beverage, Mrs. Beverage!" they shouted. "Louisa" they might have tried if they had known her as such. But no one did. Downstreet they simply called her "the captain's wife."

"Go answer," I urged her finally. "Must be important."

She wrung a fist of water from her hair. With her skirt pulled tight around her knees, she hobbled down the wharf. I caught up to her and she stopped dead still. "Nora Beverage, you stay put. This once."

The townsfolk fell silent and made a path for Mama.

At the *Veto*'s side she refused a boost from one of the crew. She hitched herself over the side and disappeared below with Father. The storm blew in fresh gusts until the crowd turned back against the wind and huddled together.

It was barely five minutes more before Mama reappeared. On deck, alone. She climbed off the *Veto* and marched headlong at me, paying heed to no one on the way.

"He's bringing them home," she announced. Her voice sank heavy in her throat. She took my hands. "I need you to help me now, Nora. We have got to make ready."

"How many, Mama?" I asked.

"Four. Only. He wants to bring them home. There were some others," she said. "He could hear them. They never came above. The rest—some crew—got off in the jolly boat and that dory we saw. But he couldn't take after them. Not into open water. The Lord will spare them if they're worthy. Otherwise . . ."

Mama stared back at the *Veto*. She tilted her face full into the storm. "This will break by dawn. Can't blow like this forever." She tugged at my hands. "Come, Nora, let's make a start. We need to hurry some."

"I'm coming, Mama." I ran from the bait shack, up the landing, and toward home. Mama half near trotted right behind me all the way.

I stoked the fire and Mama cleared the beds. She pulled the mattresses to the floor. We made a palette by the fire. Then we dried off some and Mama put a fresh dress on, but I put on my nightgown. I went to the door and opened it a crack to listen for voices. A gust blew up and the door flew from my hands. It slammed back hard on its hinges and brought Mama fast.

"That will do just fine to have the storm inside and uninvited, won't it?" Mama pulled the door to and latched it shut.

"But they'll be coming soon," I pleaded.

"I will hear them, Nora. I can let them in."

"And me too, Mama," I tried.

Mama held her hand, palm flat against the door, like she could feel them coming through its wood. Her other hand reached out to unpin my braids. "You brush these out and get to bed. These drafts can bring the fever. I think you are old enough to understand that. Well?"

Mama pulled her lips together tight. It meant I had better understand real fast and make no answer. It meant the talk was done. Ever since Owen, Mama used the threat of fever like a hickory branch.

It was time to surrender. "If you need me, I'll . . ."

"You will be in bed. Asleep." Mama flew around the house like a moth. She answered over her shoulder. "Someone needs to rest. I will need you more tomorrow."

"Won't Father want to . . . see me first?"

"It will have to be upstairs. Now go." She pushed me toward the stairs, past the table where the hairbrush rested, bristles up, still on its ivory back.

EIGHT

I sat in bed. The wind roared and settled outside. Beneath it came a lowing sound, traveling up the scale from animal to human. It broke in a sob, breathless and high pitched, a woman's voice.

I twisted into my bed and pulled the covers up.

The door slapped to downstairs. Wind blew up and visited my room. Then came my father and his crew, their heavy boots grinding and restless on the floor below. Mama said something and Father answered in a murmur. Other voices joined in, low and soft. Beds scraped some more. Then steps tramped up the stairs to my room. I lifted the covers and smelled fire, more like ashes really, sweet and stale and smoky.

Through the covers, a hand nudged at my hip.

"Pud? Puddin'? I'm home."

I threw back the covers and sat up. "Father, we were so afraid, and then we saw the *Veto* . . ."

"Sssshhhhhh, not now. We need to borrow your bed."

Finally, in the dark room, I could see that he was holding something. It took both arms, it was wrapped in canvas, it had two pale feet sticking from it.

"Here, Nora, take this for the floor." Father tilted

one shoulder toward me. It held a quilt folded into a thick square. I took the quilt and spread it on the floor. Father unrolled the canvas and stretched a body on my bed. From inside his coat he pulled a knife. I took his wrist in both my hands and clamped on tight. The blade flashed in the dark.

Father wrapped his free arm around my waist and pulled me tight against him. "Nora, let go. We've got to cut his britches off is all. He's been burned some here against the leg." He pointed with the knife. "He needs to be up here. With you. Away from the others."

I squeezed Father hard and kissed him welcome home. He tasted salty, and of smoke. "I'm just thankful you're home again for now. I wish it were for good." What I really wished was that it were December. I wished the Thorofare were froze hard as granite and wouldn't break till Judgment Day. But I didn't say so. I just held his wrist that much the harder and then let go.

I knelt and studied the boy's face, pie-shaped and soft, with a flattened nose and doughy cheeks and no real chin. His mouth fell open like a loose pocket, slack and gulping for breath.

I tugged at the tail of Father's coat. "Is he dying tonight?" I asked.

"Not tonight," Father answered. He slipped the britches in tatters from the boy's legs. "Not tomorrow neither, nor soon, I hope. He's overcome is all."

"So aren't we all," I whispered, and forced a smile.

Father never saw. "But not like this. See here." Father backed away and pulled the covers to the boy's chin, covering him except for his right leg, which stuck out naked along the edge. From above the knee to the ankle his leg shone raw and wet, blistering like scalded milk.

Well, I had seen Father skin a deer and dress it down, and pigs before curing—all peeled and shining and naked of their hide. But this was part of a live boy, a leg attached to a boy as much alive as me. I had to look away.

Father put the knife down and produced a bottle from his pocket. "This is the balm," he said, drizzling its contents along the boy's leg. "I'll leave it here by the bed, should you need it. For him. Otherwise, best give him leave to sleep, allow the leg to drain."

He stoppered up the bottle and set it at the foot of the bed. The scent of aromatic oils rushed like a sweet wind into my head.

Father caught me as I swooned sideways from my knees. He pulled me to the quilt and laid me down, doubling it over top. His strong fingers found my forehead, smoothing my hair flat out against the quilt.

"No braids this time, huh, Puddin'? Try to sleep now. If the boy stirs, call us. Your mother and me'll be right downstairs with the others." He raked his fingers through my hair like a rough comb.

"It's still wet, it's so wet, Nora," he wondered.

"I told you, Father. We saw it, all of it. You, the

Royal Tar. We were watching off Coombs' Point. We saw it all."

"No, not all of it, I fear." He kissed me along the ear, creased the quilt beneath my head, and started down the stairs.

NINE

"Who are you, anyhow?" came the small voice.

I sat up stiff from the cold floor. The quilt tumbled to my knees.

"Who are you? What are you doing here?" he asked. He propped himself up in my bed, on one slight elbow. His round face hung in the gray light of morning through the window.

"My name is Nora Beverage," I told him. "This is my room. You are in my bed. My father saved you from the *Royal Tar* last night, and brought you here."

"Is this Portland yet? We're supposed to get to Portland first, then home to Boston. Poppa's due back soon. We are meeting his ship."

"Your poppa has a ship, eh? Well, so's mine. The cutter *Veto*, and he's the captain."

"Mine too, the captain. He owns part and gets the biggest share. They go to China. Does yours go to China too?"

"Not China," I told him. "Just Castine and Blue Hill and north as far as Quoddy Head."

"China is another country, way out around the Cape." He paused and stared at my ceiling, like it might have charts pinned against the boards. "Along the Patagonia coast. They got tea there, and silk, and they braid their hair there."

"Mama does mine too," I said.

"No, not you, not girls"—he said *girls* like it was a low, common oath—"I mean the menfolk, gentlemen and traders braid their hair."

"Well, I have never seen a man like that, nor even a boyyyy." I drew out boy with some disgust just for a payback. I felt my hair. It had dried during the night and scrambled like a nest.

"But do you got dragons?" he continued. Suddenly his eyes opened wide and round as his face. "They got dragons over in China, bushels of 'em, firebreathers that can cut you with their tails, and green ugly scales big as dollar pieces. Toenails sharp as icehooks and—"

"I suppose your poppa has seen these dragons, eh?"

"Not seen, not yet. The traders can't go but in the port. The dragons live high up in the mountains. But he did bring me a chest from China, all carved over with dragons. It's got a proper dragonhead handle at each end too—a double-headed dragon whittled so's its tongues come out and twist togetherlike."

"What's your name, boy?" I asked him.

"Zenas Banks, and I'm going on eight," he said, trying to hitch himself up higher on his elbow.

"You'd better lie down some, Zenas Banks," I said. He fussed at the covers and bent from the waist. He tried to swing his leg over the bed to the floor. But his right leg just hung stiff. He pinched his round eyes shut. His mouth fell open and his lips tightened back against his teeth. One front tooth was missing; the other was halfway in.

I pushed against his shoulders and he fell down flat on the bed. He tried hard to conjure a scream, but it rattled in his throat, stuck, and faded.

"Make it stop burning, please." His eyes watered. He reached for the leg with both hands. I had to push him back to the bed. With one arm across his shoulders I pinned him down. With the other I stretched to reach the balm where Father had left it on the floor.

"Stay put," I ordered. "We'll put this on the leg—it might help." His leg had puffed up some overnight, blistering and red and shiny. I couldn't bear to look, but I did.

"There," I said. I held the stopper in my teeth and tilted the bottle over his leg. The balm covered his leg like a glaze. I tried to make a smile around the stopper, but he wasn't watching. He clung to the bedstead above his head with both hands. "Don't move a lick, Zenas. I'll be right back."

I hurried downstairs. Father and Mama slept side by side near the fire. I tiptoed past and found the rock crystal candy where I'd left it near the basin. When I got back upstairs, Zenas was still clamped tight to the bed. But his good leg thrashed beneath the covers until the bed shivered on the floor.

"Be still, Zenas. Here's some rock candy. Put it in your jaw, chew slowly and get more sweetness from it."

Zenas opened one skeptical eye and then his mouth. His jaws closed over the candy. He ground at it, crunching it like glass between stones.

"More?" he asked.

"Later, Zenas, if Mama lets me go to the store downstreet. Does your leg feel better now?"

"Feels like hellfire," he answered. "Pure hellfire."

I loosened his hand from the bedframe and slipped it in mine. He squeezed so hard, it near broke my knuckles.

Then, both his eyes opened full up. "Mama," he said. "What did you say about Mama?"

"That she might let me go downstreet later, for the candy." Then I remembered it was Sunday. Maybe Mr. Staples would make an exception, just this once.

But Zenas was remembering something else. "Not yours, Nora. Mine. My mama? Why can't she come see me?"

"Where? I mean, she was with you, Zenas, on the *Royal Tar?*"

"Of course she was. All the way from St. John, from my Uncle Eleazar's. He wanted us for the summer and we decided to stay on for an extra while. She couldn't bear to rush back to Boston just to wait for two months more. Not until the *Sully Empress* was due back in port. That's my poppa's ship. She's a three master, square rigged, a wonder of a ship."

I asked him to tell more about the *Sully Empress,* but he wanted to talk of the *Royal Tar* instead. They had sailed Friday morning. They got off late, Zenas said, because the collection had to be loaded first. All the passengers had to wait around some, he explained, sitting dockside atop their trunks for comfort.

"Loading the collection?" I interrupted.

"The Burgess Collection of serpents, birds, and exotic beasts," Zenas said, waving his hand in the air like he was writing it all down on an invisible slate. He told how they took the ones in cages first—two lions, one tiger, one leopard. They led the gentle ones down below next with ropes—the horses, six in all, two dromedaries, and the elephant came last.

"But no dragon?" I said.

"No, nor no snakes, neither. That was just how they called themselves." He was genuinely grave about it all.

"And no birds?"

"Just so many. Pellitans is how they called them, I think."

"White ones with great strange bills?" I asked.

"White and brown, that too."

"Then I saw them," I said. "I saw them, the pellitans, flying right from smoke, right when the *Royal Tar* clove right in half and sank."

But Zenas ignored me. He began talking instead about the fire. He had gone below, to the hold where they kept the animals up front. His mama had fallen asleep. Other passengers were cooking supper late. He stood outside the bulkhead, listening for their sounds, thinking how maybe a keeper would appear and let him take a look.

"And that's when it hit, the storm. She rolled flat out like we'd taken a hit from broadside. I could hear the cages shifting and grinding on the floor. And you'd never heard such a holy uproar as them animals putting up a fuss, all kinds of growling and roaring and squawking. I took hold of the ladder against the bulkhead. A sour smell came down the passage. I go up, and lo"—Zenas pinched his nose and frowned at the memory of it—"there's black smoke, too thick to see or breathe, and folks runnin' and screamin'. I try crawling up to find Mama, but everyone's going the other way and they push me out and haul me along, up above, and that's when I see the fire comin' up the hatches so I grab a capstan and hold on. There's men lowering away over the side, and then the deck's clear. I remember the deck burning and running through it and just hopin' I'm clear into the water—"

"And that's when my father rescued you, aboard the *Veto*," I finished for him.

"Did he now? I can't say." Zenas pulled the covers across his mouth and nose and stared like a robber at the ceiling. "And was there others?" came his voice, small and shy, muffled beneath the blanket.

"Some," I answered. "Some few others, but I don't know who."

"What others, and where?" Zenas brightened.

"Downstairs, some sleeping in my mama and father's own bed, but I don't know . . ."

"Downstairs, sleeping." Zenas considered, and laid his head back flat against the mattress. "Mama," he said real soft. Then, loud enough to raise a spirit, "*Mama, Mama,*" he whooped, and let it roar throughout the quiet morning of our house.

TEN

I clapped a hand over his mouth. The stairs creaked and Mama shuffled into the room.

"He's awake, Mama," I said, standing clear of the bed.

"I could tell," Mama answered.

"This is my mama," I told Zenas.

"I wanted my own one," Zenas said. Mama knelt by the boy and felt of his brow. "You got scratchy fingers," he complained. "My mama's fingers are long and . . ." Zenas couldn't finish. He twisted into the bed with pain. His eyes shut, his mouth clenched to stifle a scream.

"Could you eat something?" Mama asked. Zenas didn't say.

"Nora, run bring those biscuits from last night—and bring the raspberry," Mama ordered.

"Nunnnnhhh," Zenas grunted.

"Then what, boy?" Mama's hands smoothed at his brow once more. Once more Zenas flinched at her touch.

"His name is Zenas Banks, Mama," I explained.

"Zenas Callendar Banks," Zenas corrected, speaking with his teeth clamped shut.

"Nicely named," Mama said, "mightily distinguished."

Again Zenas pushed Mama's hand from his forehead. "It was my mama's name. Before Papa. And she wouldn't give me no hard biscuit for breakfast. She'd give me pie, a wedge as big as this"—Zenas held his hands above the covers and made a triangle with his chubby fingers—"and she'd smother it in cream so deep." And then his fingers pinched off a three-inch thickness of invisible cream.

"We will see about that." Mama stood and walked to the foot of the bed. She studied Zenas' leg. "And where did you say your mama lives, Zenas Callendar Banks?"

"Boston," he answered. "Commonwealth of Massachusetts." Mama pulled the covers off Zenas' good leg and kneaded on his foot. "Can't she come see me up here?" Zenas asked. "Can't she come up here? Nora says she is down the stairs, and I expect she'll be wanting to see me."

Mama flashed a mean look at me. I shook my head. "I only said there was passengers, I didn't say . . ."

"No matter what you didn't say," Mama snapped.

"She was on board last night, on the *Royal Tar*. I didn't mean . . ." Again, Zenas couldn't finish. But Mama wasn't listening. She flicked my dress off the peg where I had hung it. She flung it full in my face.

"Get that on and go haul water. Carry in some wood. Be of some good service, Nora Beverage. I will tend to the boy."

I was on the top step with the dress half over my head when I heard Zenas ask, "Could you make it stop hurting, please, Mum?" and Mama answered, "It won't stop until you get used to it first."

"It had better," Zenas said. "You had better make it stop." I had never heard anyone threaten Mama like that before or since. I was only glad I wasn't there in the room to see her stiffen, to see her eyes grow dark.

Downstairs I put on Mama's coat and slipped by Father sleeping near the fire. Outside was a fair sad mess. The wet grass had been flattened into mats and creased this way and that like that part in a schoolboy's hair. Tree limbs were scattered everywhere. Dead black apples, too high up to pick, had been torn loose. They stank like cider gone bad. The storm had blown on by, pulling the sky low and tight and gray behind it. A snow sky, some little bit too early.

I hauled three trips in all, enough to fill two basins and the sink. Back outside, I saw the woodshed hadn't done its job. I had to poke around some underneath to find two armloads that hadn't gotten wet like the rest. I stacked the wood inside by the fireplace and hurried out again as Father twisted on his back and yawned.

Around front of the house there was fish everywhere. The flake had splintered and caught in the rose hips. I pulled it out and stacked it against the house. I went next to picking up the fish. They weren't much good, hardly smelled like cod, rainsodden through and through. I heaved them back into the Thorofare.

A fringe of foam lined the bank, showing where the storm tide had crept up during the night. It trembled in the breeze and blew away in puffs like milkweed. Finally, I watched close to shore where a mess of crabs scrambled over the white meat. They tore off ribbons of the cod fish and slid backward into darker water.

With the last piece of fish still in my hand, I turned and climbed the bank, around the house, past the well, and on to the barn. Its door had slumped ajar in the storm. I pulled it open and walked into the gloom. It smelled of wet hay and ripe manure. Hay dust flew into my nose and I stopped short to sneeze, four short bursts. Mercy, our milk cow, stared sideways at me out of one brown eye. She sidled over in her stall. But she would have to wait for milking later. I pulled a bale of hay down from the rack and scattered it on the ground.

While Mercy ate breakfast, I squinted into the dark corners of the barn. I was looking for Bobbin and Spindle. I figured our misfortune with the cod could be their breakfast surprise. But first they'd have to show themselves. So I waved the fish around in the stalls, rattled the harness, and tried calling them to breakfast.

Mercy lifted her head and ogled me, hay spilling from her mouth.

"Just mind yourself, Mercy," I scolded. I climbed the ladder halfway to the loft and listened. Nothing, until when I turned to look down I saw them rubbing against the rough wood at the ladder's foot.

"Can't even say 'good morning,' ill-mannered cats." I dropped the fish down to them. "Might as well be of some good use," I scolded them. I smiled to hear my voice echo in the quiet barn, how much it sounded like Mama's.

Bobbin and Spindle tumbled over each other to get at the cod. They pawed the fish and smelled it and circled it again and again. When they decided it was safe, they settled at opposite ends and set to nibbling. They ate their fill and poked at the rest. I slowly came down from the ladder. They ignored me, preening and grooming, too vain to notice.

"Ungrateful cats," I scolded Bobbin. I pinched him behind the neck and pulled him to me. "I know how to civilize you, old Bob. Come on." I wrapped him in my coat. His orange head stuck out, its top fur twisted into raggedy wet knots.

Spindle stared up, puzzled, and Bobbin complained by sinking his claws into my arm.

"Mind your manners, Bobbin. I know someone who needs a friend. We're going visiting, going to pay a call. And Spindle, your turn will come. For now you're staying here."

And Spindle didn't budge a single inch.

ELEVEN

When I got back inside, Father was kneeling by the fire, stirring the ashes with a poker. A woman sat watching him from across the room. She was settled in Mama's high-backed rocker. She wore Mama's dressing gown and best gingham sunbonnet.

"Out early this morning, eh, Nora?" Father asked. "And how are the animals? Fit and sound, I hope?"

"Mama sent me out," I explained. "The animals are fine. Mercy looks eager." Bobbin clawed underneath my coat.

"Did the boy sleep last night?"

"Zenas, his name is. Yes, some, but fitful. I think it was his leg that woke him. It seems to hurt some fierce. I put the balm on him and he started to holler for his mama. I thought maybe she would be a . . . downstairs guest?" I stared at the woman in the chair. When I said "guest," she raised her face and smiled.

Father crunched at the ashes and stood. "Oh, I'm sorry, Nora. This is a downstairs guest, as you choose to say. But I'm afraid I can't remember . . ." He bowed in apology toward the seated woman.

"Charlotte Batchelder," the woman said. She stopped rocking and bent forward at the waist and tilted her head to the side. "Delighted to make your acquaintance, Nora."

"Miss Charlotte Batchelder, that's right," Father repeated. "I am sorry, Miss Batchelder."

"Not Batchelder," I said. "He's a Banks, not a Batchelder." I pointed to the closed door at Father's back. "Do you have any Bankses in there?"

"No Bankses," Father answered. He thunked a log on the fire. It settled and hissed.

"They are two spinster sisters, Nora," Charlotte Batchelder explained. She cast her eyes over to Mama and Father's room to indicate the others still in there. "Their families are living in New York, near Saratoga. They were going to visit. They told me last night as they were taking the air. But they seemed quite spry. Once they get the smoke out of their systems, I am sure they will be fit as ever."

"Then his mother is dead," I said. I guess I wanted to hear the cold flat sound of it.

"It would seem the boy's mother perished in the tragic . . . circumstances of last night, yes," Charlotte Batchelder said. She lowered her head until the bonnet concealed all but the tip of her chin.

"Many perished, Nora," Father said. "We should be thankful that Providence saw fit to spare these few."

"But how can Zenas be thankful?" Then I felt his large strong hands on my shoulders. And I pulled away. Bobbin nested beneath my arm.

"Besides, it weren't Providence, Father. It was you,

you and the *Veto*." I retreated from Father and stepped behind Miss Charlotte Batchelder. I hugged Mama's coat tight around me, Bobbin squirming underneath. Still, Father came toward me. "Besides," I almost shouted, "what's this woman doing with Mama's gown, wearing Mama's bonnet? Does Mama know she is?" That succeeded at least in halting Father where he stood. He let the poker tap its sooty end against the floor. He watched me like he must have watched the ocean, eyes bunched tight and black, fretting into creases at the corners.

Charlotte Batchelder interrupted. Her voice was a singy song. "Nora, you should be proud of your mother's generosity in allowing this gown to me. Could you only have seen the wretched state of my wardrobe after the smoke and the immersion in your adjacent waters. And that is not to slight entirely the aroma that so unhappily saturated its every fabric and thread . . ." And on and on she went, poor thing, trying so hard to smooth the air between me and my father.

I just stared at Father and shook my head. I wanted to apologize, to him and Charlotte Batchelder as well. But how she kept on with her talking!

" . . . and as to the bonnet, well the Lord forgive me, but a woman's vanity is a small offense. Still, all the same, you have a right to know . . ." Her hands flew from her knees to under her chin. She pulled loose the ties holding the bonnet beneath her chin.

"Miss Batchelder," Father protested, "Nora doesn't have to know. You're allowed your privacy as much as any of us."

I stood above her, looking down straight on the bonnet as she lifted it slowly, peeling it almost, from the right-ear side. The skin above her ear, and back up from her neck to the top of her scalp shone bare and pink and smudged. It was covered with wisps of hair, burned close against her flesh. I could smell the singe.

"Thanks to goodness, it's only hair and will grow itself out soon. But in the meantime, a woman's vanity requires this trifling masquerade." Gently she replaced the bonnet and tied it beneath her chin.

I didn't even look at Father then; *couldn't* would be closer the truth. "I am so sorry," I blurted. "Tell her I'm sorry, Father, please do." I backed toward the stairs and found the bottom step with my heel. Only when I had mounted three steps, backward and with my eyes closed, did I turn and look to see my way ahead, and climb.

TWELVE

Mama was hardly pleased to see me back upstairs. "Now what is it?" she asked. Then, "I see you helped yourself to my coat." She was kneeling behind Zenas, holding a wet cloth to his forehead.

"Who is it now?" Zenas asked.

"Just Nora," Mama said.

I walked around to the foot of my bed so Zenas could see me without moving. "Just me," I added.

"Are they up yet, downstairs?" Zenas asked. "Are the others stirring yet?"

"No," I told him, "not yet."

Zenas closed his eyes again. Mama put her mouth beside his ear and whispered, "Do you know 'Bobby Shaftoe'?"

"Not unless he might be from Boston too," Zenas answered.

"It's a rhyme, Zenas. Nora will start it for us," Mama announced.

I loosened my arm against the coat. Bobbin was rearranging himself against my ribs. "Bobby Shaftoe's gone to sea . . ." I began.

"Silver buckles on his knee," Mama joined in, and together we finished it:

"He'll come back and marry me
Pretty Bobby Shaftoe."

"The devil take Bobby Shaftoe," Zenas moaned. Mama pulled back and turned the cloth over on his brow. "Was he a one-legged boy?" Zenas continued. "One leg, one knee. 'Silver buckles on his knee' sounds like only one. What became of the other, why don't it say?"

"The other what, child?" Mama asked.

"The other knee I mean, did they burn it off, or cut it off, or did he catch it in the lines?"

"It's a rhyme, Zenas. The boy has silver buckles, so he puts it on his knee, to fasten his breeches with, don't you suppose?" Mama looked up at me and shook her head.

"Mama, he had gold buckles on the other knee," I offered.

"You're lying, I can tell. There is no other knee!" Zenas spun his head away from Mama until the wet cloth rested on his left ear. "And besides, *my* mother wouldn't let them have my leg, not without her say-so first."

I figured now was the time to risk it, if ever there was a time. I put my right hand into the coat and took hold of Bobbin. I cradled him underneath his front legs and pulled. His claws snagged and let go of my dress.

"Zenas Banks has a caller this fine Sunday morning," I announced. "A close friend from the barn. He wanted to meet you right away."

I pulled Bobbin from the coat and dropped him flat on Zenas' chest.

"He's wet," Zenas said, but nuzzled old Bob beneath his chin all the same.

Mama fell back against the wall, holding the washcloth up above her head. "Nora Beverage," she growled, "Nora Beverage, you know better."

Bobbin curled over onto his back so that Zenas could stroke his underside. "It rattles," Zenas called out. He put his ear against Bobbin's stomach to hear better.

"He likes you. His name is Bobbin." I reached to lift Bobbin off, but Zenas held on tight. He tried to stuff Bobbin beneath the covers.

That's when Mama struck. She spun the wet cloth over her head and let it snap full into Bobbin's scrambled orange face.

"They're never to come into this house, and you know that's been ordained, Nora Beverage." She let loose with the wet cloth once more, nearer its mark. Bobbin hunched down against the covers, digging, bracing himself for the next blow. Zenas raised his left arm to ward off Mama's fury. But Mama just reached her left arm underneath of it. The wet cloth still spun in the air, in her right hand, like a decoy. Then she slid her hand beneath Bobbin. She pried him loose and lofted him across the room.

"Plaguish beast," she railed. "Never in my house, and that's how it shall stay!"

Bobbin scrambled beneath the settle against the far wall, twitching his tail against the floorboards. Zenas shrank once more into his bed. I tried to retrieve old Bobbin when Mama came around the bedside heading direct for the settle.

"How many times, how many times," she was saying to herself. Just then Bobbin tried to skitter clear and away. But Mama caught him on her foot. She snapped her ankle in the direction of the stairs and sent Bobbin scudding across the bare wood. He slid out across the landing and took flight down the stairwell. He landed feetfirst four steps from the bottom and was gone.

"I want that animal out of here for good," Mama called down the stairs as I chased after him. "And you with it, Nora, until I say otherwise."

Downstairs, Father held the door open and Bobbin flashed straight through the doorway. I followed after and Miss Charlotte Batchelder watched the whole sad affair, staring from underneath Mama's bonnet.

THIRTEEN

I didn't even bother chasing Bobbin inside the barn. Instead I turned and headed downstreet, winding around branches and puddles until I stood at the top of the landing. Three gulls stood in the middle, knee-deep in a brown pool of water, nudging their bills into the mud. I walked at them and they lifted up in a rattling of feathers. In his mouth, one gull held a spiny urchin that must have washed up in the storm tide. He circled high and downshore until he'd come above the boulders just beyond Brown's boathouse. Then he dropped the urchin with a crack like a hollow egg against the rocks. He followed it down, to pick the orange meat in private and leave the broken shell to wash away next tide.

I would stay clear of Mama for a bit, stay clear of the house entire. It felt so crowded there, Mama and Zenas up in my room, him with his burning leg and Mama with her anger, mad that he hurt so much, madder there was nothing more for her to do. I had seen that all before. And Father downstairs with Miss Batchelder and the spinster sisters still in bed, all crowded around like the feelings in my head. And nothing I could do for helpfulness, and no place to be but away.

I crossed the landing to the wharf. Its pilings had held, but just barely, so that it tilted sideways against where the *Veto* tugged at its leeward side. The *Veto* bore a long scar where its paint had rubbed raw after a night of pitching and scraping against the sharp-edged planks of the wharf.

I pulled up over the *Veto*'s side. Its deck was slick and wet and crisscrossed by a mess of storm-tangled lines. The sails hung wet and heavy, bunched along the masts like wet paper. The canvas, soaked by rain, smelled sour, rank.

I went below to Father's cabin. I would stay there for as long as needed. They would miss me later, maybe, and come looking. I was safe, always safest there, and no one ever dared intrude. It was the captain's quarters, after all, and that meant Father had to find me first.

I came near breaking a leg against a table before I found the bunk in the gloomy cabin. I dropped onto the bunk and wrapped myself in a blanket. It scratched against my cheek—wet and smelling of tobacco. I curled over sidewise and set myself to the task of sleeping. Mostly, I just listened to the sea, pondering on last night. The water slapped around the *Veto*'s hull and sloshed beneath the wharf. The *Veto* rolled and groaned, its lines whining as they strained at the pilings.

Then beneath all those noises came the plop of wood on water, plop-plopping as it came closer. Between each plop came the squeak and rattle of metal on wood, oarlocks followed by the slap of oartips against water.

I raced above to see who might be about so early of a morning. From the *Veto*'s bow I could see the thin figure of a man, standing upright in a dory, stroking backward, pushing oar over oar. The boat slid across the gray water. The man leaned and bent against the oars. The dory headed backward, stern first, toward the *Veto*, the wharf.

It was Giles, old Giles Wooster, coming straight at me.

"Hullllooo," he called. His voice rolled across the flat water. I didn't make to answer.

"Hulloo," he tried again. "Is it you, Miss Nora B.?" I stood and watched. Soon, Giles floated right below me. His dory's prow slapped against the *Veto*'s hull. "Up fresh and early, ain't ye?"

"And so aren't you, Giles Wooster," I answered.

"To my advantage, Miss," Giles said. "I was rowin' to Coombs' Point. Maybe see what's left of the wreckage. Might be some prize for your friend Giles." He stood, smiling and rocking with the boat.

"You're no better than a gull, Mr. Giles Scavenger."

"I suppose not." He smiled and showed his three remaining teeth. "I suppose you wouldn't want to come along, that being the case? Could use some young eyes, is all. Mine's grown frightful dull of late."

I stared at his empty grinning mouth, at his scratchy sidewhiskers and his beakish nose. Mama would be scandalized so fierce. But then she did say to get out . . .

"Half is mine, if I say yes," I shouted.

"Damn, these Beverages is tough and hard," Giles muttered. Then he lifted his face and squinted at me. "Half is yours. Now get yourself down here, girl."

And so I did. I came over the *Veto* on the wharf side and walked to the end. Giles had rowed alongside and clamped one hand to the endpost to steady his boat.

I stepped down into the dory and sat in the stern, facing Giles. He sat now and rowed facing me from the middle seat. He rowed to the middle of the Thorofare and swung the boat to eastward. We slid silently by a ledge where cormorants nested on the rocks. Their limp wings stretched out beside them, waiting for sun to dry, before they might fly again.

"Cringin', cringin' mercy, don't they stink some bad." Giles rattled his throat and spat toward the birds.

For their part, the birds just settled more on their rocks and stared. They might have spat back themselves is how they looked, if only they could muster up the spit. For my own part, I just pinched my nose shut and waited for the wind to shift. No mistaking birdlime for perfume, and those rocks was frosted dead white with it.

So old Giles just leaned into the oars. "You sharpen your eyes to the near shore," he grunted. "I'll watch behind toward Stimpson's Island."

"Are we looking for jewels, Giles?" I asked, and then it struck me something odd. I repeated it over and over, to myself at first, and then out loud: "Jewels, Giles, jewels, Giles . . ."

Giles stopped his rowing. "I'm not here for your sport, little girl." He lifted his oars from the water and held them straight out at the side. It grew dead quiet on the water. The oars dripped and Giles huffed soft as a warming kettle.

"It wasn't for sport, Giles. I meant nothing by it, only foolishness. Can we still be half shares each?"

Giles made no answer. He gulped more air and grunted. Then the oartips broke water, and squeaking and huffing and laughing and wheezing, we lurched forward once again. We came by Brown's, where skeletons of old dead boats hunched over timbers at the shoreline. We came past the Cubbyhole, now at half tide, its muddy flats dotted with the holes of clams retreating from the sun. I hadn't walked those flats since Owen. Mama forbade it, and there was no reason to go back there anyhow.

Soon we had rowed around the point and back down the Thorofare toward home.

" . . . and crowded too, I suppose," Giles was saying.

"Crowded?" I looked to Giles. He was staring at my house back over his right shoulder.

"Yes, crowded, all them folks from the steamer, must be crowded at your home, I was thinking."

"Too much for me," I allowed. I told him about Miss Batchelder and the two sisters and Zenas Callendar Banks.

Giles asked if they were all fit and vital. When I described Zenas' leg, he knotted his face and let go a slow whistle. He felt his right leg while the oar dragged in the water. The boat spun in a circle.

"But worse is his mama was on the *Royal Tar,*" I added.

"As if the leg wouldn't be hurt enough, bless the lad." And he dropped the other oar and seemed to study on his palms, callused and creased.

"But my mama's taken him over, attending on him. He is in my bed, and she with him."

"Even so? Worse and worse." He took up the oars and began rowing. I ignored that last, knowing how he felt, how they all felt, about Mama. And wishing it weren't so hard to feel otherwise.

Soon we had rowed most full up the Thorofare with hardly so much as a splinter to claim as our own. Giles refused to quit. He hove close to shore and cautioned me to watch careful. But there was nothing, nothing but the clumps of sea grape clotting the shoreline. It snagged on mussel beds like hair tangled in a comb. And here and there, remains of sea-foam, frothy as beaten egg whites, trembled in the breeze and blew free.

The wind was blowing up again. As we rounded Coombs' Point at last it hit flush against my face. I cupped my hands against my cheeks. They were chapping now, and later would begin to burn.

"Far enough," Giles hollered over the wind. He brought the boat around, rowing hand over hand. I pulled my gaze from the gray line out to sea and looked down at the black water beside the boat. We must have rowed right over where the *Royal Tar* had burned and sank, for there back to shore I could recognize the clearing on Digger's Cove where Mama and I had stood last night. I saw the low-hanging curtain of balsam limbs where we had held our lantern, the merest spark against the bright blaze of the steamer.

But as the dory came round, I watched over Giles' shoulder. Halfway from where Mama and I had stood, in a line direct to the very tip of Coombs' Point, the water broke white and washed over and around a swelling grayness rising in the water.

"Row there, Giles, that way." I pointed over his right shoulder. He held the line steady ahead and pulled at the oars. He fixed me with a weary, crazy look.

"How much farther now?" he called between strokes.

"Not much," I answered.

"What have we got, Miss Nora?"

"Something gray—and big." I watched the shape, how it swayed, boulder shaped, attached underneath to something like pilings.

And then with a twitch the gray thing fluttered out a thin strand of line, of warp. At its end the line unraveled into a wispy brush of a thing. A tail . . .

"There's a tail, Giles."

"About what? You can tell me it later, Nora dear."

"About nothing. It's not to tell," I corrected. "It's a tail. It's alive and it has a tail at its stern side."

"Does it now?" Giles cackled between breaths. "Let's both of us have a good look." Finally he twisted the dory around half broadside. He slumped over his knees, gulping in air, greedy for it. Then, sitting up with a wink in my direction, he continued, "A tail, does she say? Well, let's see this imaginary tail of yours."

But when he squinted toward the gray water at that shape with the tail, there came a hitch in his breath. Head tilted back, he sighted down his nose.

"Cringin', cringin', cringin', cringin' jeezum Jenny Virginia, will you look at that!" Giles froze in his seat. His mouth gaped in wonder.

"Row some closer," I urged. "We'll get a better look."

Giles took up the oars and rowed in very tender strokes. He spun around and gaped once more, this time over his left shoulder, maybe for a different view. And then he pronounced it a demon. "But it is a demon," he insisted. "The vast oceans hide many hideous creatures, all birthed in hell, and this be one of 'em, I warrant ye. I'll not row nowheres near it."

"Giles, you're an old fool to talk such fancy. There's never been a day you ever believed anything like hell, or demons, or any of it."

"But there's been many a night when the demons came callin' on your old friend Giles."

"And they all lived in a bottle, I'll wager, and they all was gone in the morning." Well, didn't Giles stiffen up at that! But at least I had his full attention. "Now set to rowing at once, Giles Wooster," I continued my scolding, "or I'm going overboard here and now, and when my father fishes me out you'll have to settle with him."

"Him's no problem, Nora. It's your mother what is dangerous." Giles spat once in the water. Then he rowed up slowly toward the creature, muttering lots of "cringin'" this and "cringin'" that just below his breath.

As we drew near the creature, it became no less a marvel. A giant head swiveled toward us with ears like weathered canvas, each ear drooping to a point. They hung on either side of an enormous head without benefit of any proper neck to speak of. Tapering out from the head was an eight- or ten-foot marvel of a nose crossed by creases running its entire length. It dangled and slithered and twitched almost like a separate creature, say a serpent, with a life and purpose all its own. Beside the nose curved two white teeth or horns. They grew down and out with the bend and length of the blade on a scythe.

A leather strap passed beneath the animal's mouth and up around its head. It made a sort of cap. Another strap crossed side to side above its eyes. The strap was studded with a row of brass buttons, and spelled out along the buttons in red-painted letters was the name "Burgess."

"Burgess," Giles read. "You are the ugliest, dumbest, funniest-looking thing I ever had the mispleasure of seein'."

"Burgess," I repeated, "it's Burgess. Must be the elephant. The boy—Zenas—he said the elephant came last."

"Elephant," Giles repeated, "elephant."

But Giles looked at me as dumb and mean as he had the elephant. He didn't know a thing about the Burgess Collection of Exotic Beasts, he didn't know about the two lions, one tiger, one leopard, six horses, two dromedaries, and the elephant. To say nothing of the two pellitans, which I didn't choose to mention. Giles had all he could manage.

"Do you figure he's a flesh eater, Nora Beverage?" Giles asked.

"Why don't you inquire that of Burgess?" I answered.

"Do you figure he understands the mother tongue?"

"No less than you, is how I figure."

But I think Giles was dead serious. We were no more than three full boat lengths away from Burgess now, and drifting flat in front. Giles pulled himself up to his full height. He stared straight on into Burgess' eyes. Burgess stared back. Neither gave much quarter.

"DO YOU BE A FLESH EATER, MR. BURGESS?"

Burgess lifted his strange nose in salute. Then he loosed a mournful bleat and held it so long, it rose up over the wind and roaring sea and knocked old Giles backward across his seat.

Giles sat, took up the oars and deliberated. "And how do you propose to get your half share to make a happy landfall?"

I pondered the problem. "Well, same as your half does. Neither half's much good out here. Unless we fix him with a bell to be a channel marker."

Giles rowed us around Burgess three times, getting closer with each circuit. Giles admired his skin, how it wrinkled and draped. But he showed disappointment in his tail, declaring it a poor second to a piece of frayed rope. Still, he calculated that Burgess had the strength of maybe ten or fifteen oxen hitched together. Come spring, he figured, Burgess could pull two, three plows at once and planting would be an afternoon's work. And of course Giles would profit handsomely by hiring out Burgess for a generous sum.

"Not so long as he stays stranded out here on these elephant rocks," I reminded Giles once more.

"Elephant rocks, that's highly poetical," Giles declared. "Yes, Elephant Rocks it is." With that we had given a name to that pile of low-water rocks just beyond Coombs' Point.

"But now that we got a name for it, how do you propose we get him off this rock pile?" I asked.

Giles told me to be patient, he was laying plans. He took up a coil of rope he had stowed in the dory's bow. He uncoiled a length and seemed to study Burgess' dimensions for a spell. Finally he bolted from the boat and found his balance on the ledge beneath, hip deep in water. He looped the line over the creature's head and brought it down beneath its forelegs. He fashioned a slip knot and pulled until the rope came snug beneath the elephant's chin. Burgess shivered in protest and rolled his head from side to side.

Giles reclaimed his seat in the dory. He took up the oars and rowed us toward shore. I fed out the rope, uncoiling it through my hands so fast it near burned. When the coil was all fed out, Giles produced another length from the dory's prow. He hitched the ropes together end to end and slapped the new coil at my feet.

"This too, Nora, far as we need to go." I fed that out too, and soon Giles had crunched the dory onto shore—Digger's Cove, where Mama and I had stood the night before.

"You'll be going ashore right here, Miss Nora," Giles announced. "You'll be keeping watch on Burgess until I'm back with help. Now haul that line along with you."

I eased myself overboard and picked my way

among the wet rocks to shore. I stood there dumb, with the shank end of the rope uncurling at my feet. "Do I hold him tight or play him out if he starts to get restless?"

With that, Giles leaped from the boat and took the line from my hands. In a minute he had secured its end to the trunk of the nearest tree. "That's all ye do, girl. You've naught but to stay put and fix your eyes on that creature out there. And hope he don't get restless."

"And if he does?"

"Then stand clear this tree, as I'll imagine he'll get the better of it."

With that, Giles bent hard into the oars, pulling double fast against the rugged chop, rowing west toward town.

FOURTEEN

I sat almost forever, it seemed to me. The tide lowered around Burgess until his ankles were most clear of the water. He swayed his head to and fro but stayed put. I was freezing to the bone, wet clear through. The sky lifted some and clouds tore off in nappy pieces. The sun broke clear. The wind rose and scrubbed the water, blowing cold despite the sun.

At last I heard voices across the water. I could see them coming, four, five dories, Giles out front. As they got closer I could see the last two boats towing lines, like necklaces, strung with barrels instead of beads. They finally came near Burgess and circled round him. Giles continued right toward me, standing and pushing at his oars. Smoke rose from where he stood in the boat, winding between his legs. As he came near shore I could smell hot pitch.

"We're going to float him over, Nora," Giles announced. His feet stradled a pot of hot pitch.

"With those?" I pointed to the dories trailing their lines of barrels. I breathed the smell of pitch, like swallowing a piny forest.

"You got better? I sure don't," Giles snapped. "Now you stay put. Lem Carver promised us his team to tow it in with. We'll bring the lines ashore."

Abruptly, Giles sat and rowed off to join the others. He went along the line of floating barrels, daubing at them with a stick pulled from his pitch pot.

Then I understood. They pulled those lines alongside Burgess and floated them underneath his legs. Giles stood knee-deep on the ledge and pulled the lines through. He slung the free ends over the top of Burgess and Samuel Crockett caught them from his dory on the other side. Soon they had all lines secured. Burgess was cinched tight with three corsets of barrels. They pulled back the last ones up beneath his thick gray legs, both front and back, and snugged them tight.

From behind me came a cracking of limbs. Suddenly Lem Carver appeared back up the trail, his face and beard glowing red. He was leading his two oxen by their traces. He stood huffing through his red beard, stooped beneath the weight of the oxen's yoke slung across his own shoulders. He paused to gather his breath.

Then Lem saw the line tied to the tree beside me. He followed it out with his eyes until he caught sight of Giles and Burgess standing together on the ledge.

"Oh now," Lem said. He removed his hat and stared into its crown and counted ten. He looked out once more. "Oh now, well now, now now," he repeated.

He replaced his hat and looked back at me. "That's a what now, Nora?"

"A elephant," I told him.

"Well, is it now?" Lem turned and stared back at his team, like he was measuring them, weighing them in his head. "This is something more than just your root-stuck plow, Jim. More than just another oak stump needs hauling, Cracker." He was talking to his animals. They just stamped some and looked the slightest bit disheartened. Finally, he loosed the line tied to the tree and hitched it to his team's harness. Feeling the weight tug at them from behind, the team grew restless. It was time to pull.

Lem reached above his head and broke a switch from an alder branch. "Now take this here, Miss Beverage." He offered me the switch and arranged me right beside Jim's right flank. I watched as Lem raised a thick brown hand and brought it down with a fearsome hollow clap across Jim's leg.

"See there, Miss? Jim don't queer easy, he's so thick-skinned and slow. So snap him hard when it's time."

"I will try to, Mr. Carver," I told him and swiped hard at the air beside Lem Carver's head. The switch said *wheet* and Lem flinched back like he'd caught a face full of bees.

Together we stared out across the Thorofare to where Burgess perched atop his rocks. He remained fixed and gray, a victim of much foolishness, dignified even with lines and barrels bulging from his sides. Around him now swarmed Giles and the several dories like gnats about a sickly cow. Two boats hung on either side, Giles in his dory floated out in front and stood slowly, straddling the seat. Burgess lifted his head, and I saw his small eyes roll with fear.

"Ready now, girl," Lem Carver rasped his command. I raised my switch and set my aim.

Giles raised both his hands overhead and brought them together at his waist. I counted one two three and then the sound of his clap reached me over the water, a loud crack like the report of a musket.

"Haw, Jim, Haw, Cracker!" Lem roared at the team. I heard his switch pop first and brought mine down across Jim's rump.

"Pull, haw, pull hard, boys!" The oxen trampled the ground, got purchase, and leaned into the line. It pulled taut, cleared the water its entire length, and set to humming with the strain. A veil of spray fell from the line. Out on his rock, Burgess balked at the force of the pulling line. He fell back upon his haunches. He rolled his head up and back, rattled his ears, and lifted his long nose above his head. The line pulled around his neck, tighter and tighter, and I feared he would strangle.

Suddenly Jim and Cracker got the advantage. They lurched forward and I looked back in time to see Burgess surrender his head to the force of their pull. He stuttered to the rock's edge, his toes caught. He tumbled into the ocean with a rolling *smack!* The wash and spray of his fall shot a plume barn high and vanished in the wind. On either side a steep and rolling wave threatened to scuttle all the dories.

Slowly then from the wash rose Burgess, bobbing with his corset of barrels and lines. His small eyes shone dark with fear. Just as suddenly the barrels began to slip and tangle. Soon the barrels had arranged themselves along Burgess' right flank and over his back like clots of barnacles. Still Lem drove the oxen. Giles rowed in a fury beside Burgess, but there was nothing to be done. Burgess rolled to the side and listed slowly over like some hull-shot schooner. As he sank slowly into the Thorofare, the lines floated free. From beneath him the barrels broke and exploded off the water like grease off a skillet. Straining till the very last to keep his head above water, to keep his long nose pointing in the air, he sank in a froth beneath the gray-black water and was gone.

"Whoa, boys, go easy now!" Lem called to his team to halt. He next produced his knife. But when he made to cut the line free, I caught at his wrist and twisted.

"Let go of it, girl," he protested, pulling his arm away. "Giles knew I would have to cut it free. It's gone and it's not taking my team with it."

"It's your team, but not your elephant," I answered.

"Nor yours neither," Lem said.

"Will be!" I shouted. Lem set the blade against the line and began to saw. I lifted my alder switch against him, ready to bring it down full hard across his shoulders.

"Give me that thing before you break them oxes' backs," Lem ordered. "Now leave 'em to me. You go back, stand watch."

Lem turned back to the line with his knife, but to no purpose. The sinking weight of Burgess and the force of the oxen planted on the trail and straining back against the line proved too much. The line snapped. It flew by my head, trailing a tail of salty spray. It snapped at Lem and knocked him backward in the mud. The line whipped back against the oxen and they staggered backward and lumbered away down the trail. Lem found his legs and disappeared after them.

Out on the water Giles lay down in his boat and hung his head over the prow. He stared into the tar-black water and waited. I waited with him from the shore, watching nothing. Then, from the bow of Giles' dory broke a spray across the water, like the blowing of a whale. Giles got a soaking and rolled over on his back to discover the source. It blew again, a fan-shaped veil of water at the surface. Gray and serpentine, it broke the surface and blew once more. The gray thing rose still farther from the water, twitching, reaching for the air. Its nose—his nose, that long creased nose of Burgess—inch by inch it lifted up, drawing closer to the shore. Giles scurried about in his boat, when at last out of the water came Burgess' head. Just behind, Giles stood in the boat and whooped halloo. I whooped back, then saw Burgess' back lift clear the water, carrying Giles and the dory with it. The boat flipped, and Giles hurtled into the air, arms and legs spinning wildly. Giles splashed clear and disappeared under the water.

Giles bobbed to the surface and flailed about beside Burgess. Hardly fifty yards from shore, but deep enough to drown. Mama had told stories of men younger and stronger drowning on the mudflats when the riptide pulled them down. Giles probably had heard even worse. Frantic, wide-eyed with fear, he saw his only chance and made straight for Burgess. He beat at the water with his arms and stayed just barely afloat. Finally, he caught hold of the strap across Burgess' head and hoisted himself up. He straddled Burgess' neck and made snug his legs on either side.

"Hold tight, Giles," I hollered. "He's swimming, he can swim after all." Sure enough, Burgess was swimming like a pup tossed in a pond. His head thrust forward, he pumped his legs and strained against the water. Slowly, he moved forward, Giles slumped across his neck. At last the animal found bottom and stood shoulder high in the water. He clambered across the rocky bottom in toward shore. He flapped his giant ears while Giles picked rockweed from beneath the leather strap.

"We did it, he's ours for good!" I yelled up to Giles.

Giles made no answer. He was too caught up in breathing and clutching at the creature's neck to realize he was safe. There stood Burgess, still up to his haunches in water, ready to make landfall but in no apparent hurry. Giles still sat upright, triumphant at last and dripping wet all the same. "Well, Miss Beverage, we salvaged ourselves a prize. It's a fifty share for the both of us."

"Hadn't you better get down from there, Giles?" But they were still in maybe three feet of water and Giles looked disinclined. I seized on the rope and tried to coax Burgess all the way up on land. He rolled that head and sniffed across the water, filling the air with a burst of gusty snorts.

Again I tugged, and this time Burgess crept obediently ashore. He made a glad landfall, stood ever so delicate among the rocks, and bleated through that twisting, curling nose.

"Ain't she a fair cunnin' wonder of a creature," called Giles down from his perch. He stroked Burgess like a baby infant just above the ears. That near-toothless grin cracked a black hole in Giles' face and his eyes near disappeared behind his bulging cheeks.

"You ought to be getting down," I tried again.

"All in due course," he answered. "I think this feller here is partial to my company."

"He would be the first," I answered. Giles wiped at his nose to hide the grin creasing his face.

I ignored him and came up beside Burgess. Gently, so as not to startle him, I raised a hand beneath his mouth. I felt of those two curving teeth growing out from under where his nose began. They were smooth and hard and white and cool as water. Burgess hardly seemed to mind my touch. I let go and stepped back. But from behind I felt a squeeze. Burgess had caught me with his nose. It came over my shoulder and down across my waist. It tugged me backward two, three steps and squeezed again, a gentle hug, and then let go.

"Seems he's a little tender for you too, dear," Giles teased.

I grabbed Burgess' rope and tugged. We marched off together. Giles had no chance to dismount. Burgess pushed through the close trees. Bare sharp branches scratched and broke against his sides. We hardly noticed. Giles, so high up, caught some weepers across his face. He dodged and bobbed and cussed blue sparks at the air around him. Burgess kept on, smashing rotted blowdowns with his feet, rolling his head side to side and pushing forward down the trail with his nose.

Finally the trail widened and we reached the road. There stood Lem with his team, and behind him maybe half the island. They whistled and whooped and hushed and scattered in bunches. Thayer Parker and his mother hid behind a tree. Dogs barked. The Cooper boys stood bold as jays in the middle of the road.

I tugged again and Burgess kept on walking. The townsfolk cleared a way. They stood alongside the road and gaped. Giles sat fast on his perch and waved broadly to all who watched. Lem stayed close in front to have some of the glory for himself. It grew quiet as a church. We reached near home. Father stood at center road, the barn behind his back. He was waiting for me.

"And what do you propose we do with that?" he shouted at last.

We drew closer. "It's an elephant," I told him. "From the *Royal Tar*."

"No doubt," he said.

"Half mine, half your Nora's," Giles offered from on top of Burgess.

"Whyn't you get down from there, Wooster," Father called back.

"Not likely very soon," Lem Carver broke in. "Giles thinks he's found a home."

Father studied Giles some while, then watched as Lem hitched his team to a tree. "And what's your part in this, Giles Wooster?" he asked.

"Your Nora helped me haul him in," Giles answered.

"That so, Nora?" Father asked.

"It's so," I answered. "We drove Lem's team, and pulled Burgess off the ledge, to shore."

"Burgess?" Father spun around, looking, then seemed to understand. "Oh, Burgess, is it?" He stared at the elephant and almost cracked a smile.

By now folks had gotten bold enough to pull in close behind of Burgess. They listened to Lem and Giles and smiled, expecting nothing different. Some edged up to Burgess' legs. Young Mason Cooper with his crooked nose flickered at Burgess' tail and took hold. He held it straight out like a shank end of rope and twirled. "Looky at this, boys," he called, "ain't no more than a sorry brush to whisk flies."

All hands laughed save me and Giles. Father took my arm and pulled back toward the barn. Giles swiveled around and climbed across Burgess' back. He flattened out spread eagle across those huge gray haunches. He uncurled an arm toward Mason and shook a fist till it blurred.

"Don't dare to touch us, boy. Touch nothing or I'll have your hand. You're a wretch and a baggage and you'd best get scarce real fast or I'll be comin' down to see you." Giles near slid headfirst into the crowd. Mason Cooper disappeared behind a wall of brothers and cousins. Giles inched his way back on top of Burgess' neck. There he squatted on his knees and gave a look that hung fire. He sat wet and slick, his yellow-gray hair now almost green as weed. He stiffened his back and threatened once more: "And that applies in the general sense to you all. This creature belongs to me now, to me and Miss Nora Beverage there, a half share each. And we'll not endure a trespass of our beast. We saw 'im first, we saved 'im, we hauled 'im in, and now he's ours. Ours to do with as we please."

"You mean a pot of stew to feed the island," came a voice.

"Elephant stew until June," came another. The crowd rippled with laughter.

"Elephant chowder," another voice added and the laughter became a roar.

"Chowdah, chowdah, gray as gunpowdah," another voice mocked. And they pulled away from us, from Burgess, now lost in their own delight, and their new rhyme, and their glee with making all into a mock.

Giles sat high and wet and stern, refusing to look after them. Again, Father pulled at my arm. "Come, Nora. You'd best get inside for now. Dry off and dress warm. It's not been easy in there either. We need to be quiet."

"Why do they treat him so, Father?" I had to ask.

"Giles? Seems that maybe he invites it. It's cruel, some, but they would always find someone—if not Giles, then someone. Of course, he did put on a show, him and that creature."

"But he's not like that, not always." I remembered Giles alone in the boat, quiet and halfway sad.

"Most folks see Giles as a useless old man. Has no one but his drink and a few old mates to share it with." Father paused and watched Burgess shifting where he stood. Giles seemed untouched. He watched over the tops of trees to the open water of the Thorofare.

"See him up there," Father continued in a whisper. "He's got himself something at last, something no one else here's ever had. All men like to have a measure of standing. Old Giles has never been much good for anything, as long as I can recall. Now he's got that unfortunate creature, he feels he counts for something."

"Don't forget, a half share is mine, Father," I reminded him. "I guess that gives me standing too."

"You, my Puddin', are full up with standing already." Father brushed my hair with his lips. He squeezed my arm and steered me to the house. "Now get inside. I'll see to Giles and Burgess, whatever in the world. Just get inside, and be careful."

FIFTEEN

Sunday morning was spent by the time I got in the house. The afternoon moved slowly. I felt no more than a city beggar locked inside the poorhouse. Upstairs Mama kept a watch on Zenas. I tried going up to see, but she shooed me like she had the cats. She made a furious steamy noise with her lips and flapped the backs of her hands until I retreated down the steps. Downstairs again, I greeted Miss Batchelder, still wearing Mama's bonnet. She fussed in the kitchen. Mama appointed her—not me—to begin the supper. She washed a cabbage and tore it leaf from leaf to soak. She started a hard dry piece of brisket to simmer by the fire. Downcellar she fetched seven apples. She cored them and set them in a pan.

I filled the apples with sugar and put them in to bake. Miss Batchelder asked me to visit the sisters and freshen their water. I had almost forgotten them, truth to tell. I cracked the door to Mother and Father's room and peered in. Both lay stiff and crooked in the great bed, back to back. I stepped in quietly but woke them both.

"Goodness, what a beauty," the right-hand sister said. At that they both sat up and settled against the headboard. Both were wearing Father's nightshirts. Both were wispy, white hair tangled round about their faces. Both fixed their hands atop the covers, folded together shyly above their laps. Their hands were yellow, papery, the skin stretched tight across their knuckles. I introduced myself and curtsied.

"Nora, that's a lovely name," the one said.

"Just delightful," added the other.

"You must be proud of your father," said the first.

"A fine man, brave and handsome," the other said.

"He is, I am, thank you both," I answered.

They were the Putnam sisters, Cornelia and Elizabeth, from Portland and returning from a stay at their brother's in St. John. He had a granddaughter named Cornelia Elizabeth. She favored her mother, they said, in her fairness and her indolence. They imagined she was just about my age. When I told them I was twelve, they clucked and apologized. Cornelia Elizabeth was only ten. What's more, she was only barely ten at that. They had given her a pendant in September for her birthday. I couldn't imagine how they could be so far wrong. Barely ten to nearly thirteen is a remarkable distance to gauge wrongly.

From the table beside the bed I lifted the pitcher and basin. "I will bring you fresh water," I said. The pitcher still seemed most full.

"That's wonderful." The sisters nodded together and smiled.

"Supper will be soon," I added.

"Cabbage, I expect," said the first sister. She inhaled deeply, and so did her sister. So did I, and the strong, steamy smell of cabbage filled us all with appetites.

"And brisket with the cabbage, and roasted apples, and more," I added.

"It would be good to dress and join you, but alas," the second sister pined.

"I will see to clothes for you," I told them. "Sure, you are welcome to join us all the same. But I will talk to Mother." Then I turned toward the door, balancing the full pitcher in front.

"Isn't she wonderful?" said one sister.

"She certainly is that, I'll warrant you," finished the other.

I pulled the door to and filled the pitcher in the kitchen. Miss Batchelder stooped by the fire, pushing a spoon at the cabbage. She said to warn Mama supper would be served when the cabbage was done. I stood near the oven to smell the apples better, and to feel the heat. Miss Batchelder chided me for lingering.

Mama caught me at the top of the stairs and shooed me halfway down. Her skirt was matted and wrinkled, her hair undone. The right side of her face was creased and flushed red. She had been sleeping, maybe only lying, in the bed with Zenas, I could tell.

"Don't come tramping up here"— she pointed back at my room—"without the merest excuse to make yourself a bother. Now what is it?"

"Miss Batchelder said to tell you supper will be soon . . ."

"Tell Miss Batchelder to serve the sisters and your father and herself. And you, of course. You can fix the boy a bowl if he wakes. I have no appetite, myself." She sighed mightily and turned to mount the stairs.

"Did you tell him yet, Mama?" I asked.

She spun. Her face twisted with puzzlement.

"The boy, Zenas?" I tried again. "About his mother, I mean. Did you tell him his mother . . . perished in the fire on the steamer, when it sank last night?"

Mama stared me down the stairs. Her face showed only bewilderment, as though I spoke in Biblical tongue. And then it faded, that look, until her creases smoothed. She managed a smile, the frosty one she reserved for greeting island folk. "Nora, we don't know the full of it quite yet. There will be time for finding out and telling what we have to tell. The boy has other burdens now. You'd best tend to your affairs downstairs." Abruptly then she disappeared beyond the landing. I stood fixed halfway down the stairs and listened.

Slowly, with a low groan of wood and rope, my bed yielded under her weight and settled.

Downstairs, Miss Batchelder was setting out bowls and silver. I told her Mama and the boy would not be down, but to set out a bowl for Father. I returned the pitcher to the sisters. They asked again about the loan of a gown or two to join us for supper. I told them Mama was indisposed and otherwise troubled by events in my room. The best I could offer them was blankets, off their own bed and from the chest at its foot. They made chirping sounds of shock and embarrassment, but in another minute they both were wrapped in blankets, moving around the room like ghosts. They trailed me into the kitchen and floated near the fire.

"Hello, Miss Putnam; Miss Putnam, good afternoon," Miss Batchelder greeted them. They begged to be useful and Miss Batchelder set them to chores. I rescued the apples from the oven. The Putnams circled the table, fussing at the cutlery, placing salvers here and there. The room boiled with steam, some smoke, the cabbage mixing with the cooling apples to warm the air with supper and the smell of food. Windows misted over, gauzing the faint gray light still left outside. I lit the lamps, and the sweetness of the oil burning joined the rest. Miss Batchelder lifted the cabbage from over the fire and near dropped it on her shoes. I returned the pot to its hook and swung it away from the flames. We spooned the cabbage into bowls. The sisters sat, still fretting at the arrangements of knives and spoons. They first lifted a salver, then jumped a spoon, slid the salt mill to the center, moved all four bowls around the table, place to place. It seemed a game I didn't know, perhaps checkers played without a board.

Ceremonies done, we sat to eat. Miss Batchelder offered grace, something full of "bounty" and "bestows." It must have been Methodist. Amen done, Miss Batchelder set to slicing the brisket. We passed the platter and took each a slice for our cabbage. All hands set to eating and slurping, a most somber proper meal. Maybe three spoonfuls later, the Putnams pushed back their bowls and blessed Miss Batchelder for her stew. "A wonderful stew," one pronounced it. "Perfectly wonderful," the other amended. For her part, Miss Batchelder praised the brisket and offered us all a second portion. Then they began to praise the cabbage, and doubly so when I admitted it came from my own cabbage yard. To hear them go on, you'd have fancied yourself at the royal court of Louis in his prime. I nodded gratitude on behalf of my cabbage and made to clear the table.

Suddenly from outside came a roar of voices. I wiped at the kitchen window and through the blur watched Father walking from the barn. A swarm of men followed him behind, troubled and urgent. Some carried muskets. Others held pitchforks. They tried to overtake Father, but he turned and raised both arms. He shouted at them, four or five ferocious words I couldn't hear. He turned back to the house and made straight for the door. The others pulled away, muttering and unpleasant. They shouldered their weapons and marched up past the barn, a ragtag militia of farmers and fishermen. The door exploded open. I shrank to the sink as the door rattled shut and I heard the bolt slide and catch.

"Crazy as coots. No end to it, more and more. Ho, cabbage and what else? Good day, ladies, Miss Batchelder. Nora, come sit."

I joined Father at the table. Miss Batchelder and the Putnams huddled by the fire. Father stood and sat, then swiveled sideways to the table. He tugged at a boot, then dropped his foot to the floor with a sharp report.

"Can I get you the bootjack, Father?" I offered.

"I should keep them on, Nora. Help me to some cabbage would be better." I stood to fetch his bowl and serve. But Miss Batchelder appeared at the table with a steaming bowl and half the brisket. Father ate without lifting his eyes, savoring little, tasting less. I rinsed a bowl and served myself an apple. I pulled the skin away and mashed the warm fruit in its brown sweet syrup.

"You'll be wanting cream for that, eh, Nora?" Father asked.

Cream. I remembered Mercy, my morning chores cut short. "We haven't any cream, I'm afraid, Father. I forgot to milk Mercy. I will get to her soon."

"Before bursting, I am hopeful," Father said. "But take care to keep the barn shut tight. Hiram Lufkin is full of strange tales." Father drained the juice from his bowl and slid it cross the table. He studied the Putnams for permission, then continued. "Hiram Lufkin carted a ewe downstreet, all the way from up-island, up to his Beacon Head pasture. A dead ewe. Mauled and bloodied, chewed all about the throat. He claims it's something from the *Royal Tar*, some beast. Queered his flock so bad, they near half broke free. He's recovered three from Mullen's Wood is all. They wanted me to join them, hunt the creature down."

"Did he see it?" I asked. Meanwhile, Miss Batchelder and the Putnams had pulled close to the table.

"He said not, said he saw nothing. But the others convinced him maybe he had. It was moving too fast is all he can say. It was too dark. His eyes were too weak. But he was sure he saw something."

"Anything is possible in this world," Miss Batchelder offered weakly.

"What's possible is it was a bear or wolves, most likely. Don't need some beast off a steamship just to attack a wretched helpless ewe."

"There were lions, a tiger, dromedaries, and pellitans on that ship," I said. "Zenas saw all of them."

"So did we," a Putnam volunteered. "Cornelia and I watched them loading in St. John. Didn't we, Cornelia?'"

Cornelia nodded and began: "Yes, all. The tiger was a most elegant, comely creature. The lions seemed drowsy, the camels foul and loathsome. And the elephant, my goodness . . ."

"It is in our barn, the elephant, right now," Father said. As one, the three women clapped hands across their mouths and breathed in pinched little gasps. "Cramped and nearly pushing up through the hayloft, but in our barn, chewing on our hay. And this," Father continued with a nod in my direction, "this young Nora of mine is its rescuer, its salvation. Now she has only to find some purpose for this sad creature and be shut of it."

"She's marvelous, she is," Cornelia Putnam said, "just like her father, rescuers and heroes both the same."

"But lions and tigers is another matter," Father interrupted.

"But they were in cages, weren't they, dear?" Cornelia appealed to her sister. Elizabeth explained that yes, they were all in cages save for Burgess. Everyone then agreed that surely no others could have escaped the tragedy. Only Burgess, uncaged and too big to sink, could have certainly survived.

"Except for the pellitans," I added. All faces stared in my direction. "I mean, I saw them, these strange large birds, with bills sagging and drooping. They rose up over the flames and circled away. It was magnificent just to behold."

Father rose from the table and stalked back to the window. "Well, that is sufficient talk of animals and creatures and the like." He peered through the window and wiped it with his fist. "Still, no harm in being prudent for the while. Take care being out of doors, secure all bolts, and note closely any strange noises."

"What strange noises?" It was Mama, leaning on the newel post and yawning. Sleep rumpled and twisted in her skirts, she approached the table and sat. "What strange noises are we to listen for?" she persisted. Father explained about Hiram Lufkin's ewe. Mama called it more island nonsense. She was sure nothing had survived the fire save for our four guests from the *Royal Tar*.

SIXTEEN

That's when I realized Mama didn't know about Burgess. She hadn't been outside all day, nor had the others. Zenas couldn't have known either. That was two things he didn't know.

Mama went to the stove and fixed herself a bowl. She joined Father and the others at the table, where she stared into her bowl, half asleep. She poked at the food, stirring the broth with her spoon as the steam rose against her face.

"Eat something, please," Father urged her. "We have finished our portions but you must eat."

"Must, but don't know if I can," Mama said into her bowl. "Has Nora been of any use today?"

The Putnam sisters started in how wonderful I was, how helpful and how bright, how much I reminded them of their beloved Cornelia Elizabeth up in St. John. Mama seemed skeptical of their praise. Never once did she turn to notice me behind. I had become near invisible to Mama and so it seemed best to disappear for real. As Mama settled into her dinner, I stole quietly up the stairs.

Zenas lay sideways along the bed, facing the wall. His bad leg stretched behind and off the bed, where

Mama had propped his foot on top of a stool. I knelt beside the bed and placed a hand gently over the covers where his hip rose in a swell.

"Sssshh Zenas, don't move, be still. I have come to see you. It is Nora, remember? I will go if you are sleeping, just say." I waited for an answer, listening for Mama's footsteps on the stairs. After minutes he still made no answer. Finally I pushed away to rise and his hand flew from beneath the covers and trapped mine against his hip.

"No wait, don't go," he whispered. "Stay, Nora, please."

"My mother will be coming up soon," I told him. "I just wanted to see you, is all."

"Did you bring that cat with you? Bobbin, was that it, Nora?" he asked.

"Yes, it was Bobbin, but no, I didn't bring him this time. He is outside. Mama makes him stay outside, out in the barn with Spindle and the others."

"What's Spindle?" Zenas twisted backward and turned his head to me.

"Spindle is Bobbin's brother. They stay together in the barn and catch mice. But I'm not to bring them in the house, as you found out."

Zenas hardly remembered. He laid his head down onto the pillow and lifted his hand from on top of mine, running it across the wall, making smaller and smaller circles. "Do you have any?" he asked at last.

"Any what?"

"Brothers, sisters," he answered.

"No, just cats."

"I don't got any of them either," Zenas said. Then he pulled his hand from the wall. It floated above his head briefly and then settled again on top of mine. He squeezed my hand and pulled it around him in front and held it tight against his chest. "I am afraid. Your mother scares me, sometimes. I ask her anything, she answers that my leg must get better first. Leg, leg, leg, leg. She's running me like a blinkered horse and it frightens me Nora. Why don't you stay with me. I would rather it was you, Nora."

"Mama is strong sometimes, yes," I tried to explain. "I understand. But she will be just as strong for you when you need her. Don't let it frighten you and it will be better. You know I would stay if I could."

I squeezed his hand back and pulled away from his grasp. I could hear chair legs downstairs scraping across the floor, china rattling in the sink. Mama would be coming up. "I have to go now. . . ."

"Please promise you will tell me one thing," Zenas began.

I interrupted. "I will tell you one thing but it is my secret for now. It is in the barn and I will tell you soon. Now promise me you will never say anything about this visit. Promise."

"Never ever," Zenas said, making a big King's X against the wall with his hand. And then I stole back downstairs, in time to see Mama scrubbing bowls in the sink.

When she had finished, Mama asked Father to join her in their bedroom. She excused herself to the others and said she would be only a moment. They closed the door behind them. I cleared the table. I offered the ladies apples but they declined. They whispered in the corner amongst themselves. I thought of Mercy, needing milking. I would tend her later. I knew it was Zenas they were speaking of, Mama and Father.

And then they returned. Mama surprised me by hugging me firm about the waist. Father crossed the kitchen and went upstairs.

"Is he bad, Mama?" I asked.

"Do you ever miss Owen, sometimes?" Mama asked me back.

"Sometimes I do," I said. "Sometimes I can't remember Owen." I struggled to see him. Round pie face, squealing with delight, hiding the cats beneath his shirt. Only kittens then.

"I miss him all the time," she said. I suppose I knew that. Sometimes I thought that Mama had sailed off with Owen to a land far away. Sometimes I thought she would never come back—she'd been gone more days than I could ever count.

"We can't miss him all the time now, Mama." I watched her face. I went on. "It's three years since July. He doesn't belong to us anymore. Not like he used to."

"His voice was like a bell," Mama sighed. "And his temper, so wild, stormed around like the weather." She tilted back her head and watched the ceiling. Her right hand flew to her brow. She pushed at wisps that floated wild around her face.

"My temper," she added, and smiled at the ceiling.

"I mean, he isn't ours to miss that much," I tried again. "It's better to let him come and go some. Otherwise it gets to be something, well, selfish maybe." I dared to say it, yes, and readied for the sharpness of her voice, or worse.

She hadn't heard. Head cocked, she was listening to the floorboards above. With her eyes, she traced the thunk of bootheels across the groaning floor. They rattled down the steps, then Father stood silent. His face sagged. "There isn't much to do now. The leg is bad. He will rouse and endure it, or not," Father said.

"This time we will have a doctor," Mama announced. "This island is no jail, not mine anymore. I won't watch another one die. Let me pack a bag for you now."

Father pulled at his chin, measuring the stubble with his fingers. "Dr. Pickering lives in Camden. I can be there soonest."

"By morning?" Mama asked.

"By morning, yes, or sooner even," Father answered, "especially if the weather holds and the winds go steady. Of course, I can't promise Dr. Pickering will be at home."

"He will be home," Mama said. "Now you raise a crew and I will pack your bag."

Father slipped on his monkey jacket. Mama went for his bag and carried it into their room. I packed something more to eat—bacon for the crew, coffee, apples from downcellar. In a crock I found the biscuit from the night before. Father's coming-home biscuit, hard now as wishing stones. Mother returned from packing and plumped Father's bag center table. The Putnam sisters and Miss Batchelder stood stunned in a corner, watching us fly like moths around the room. Father returned, found his hat, and pulled it low across his ears.

"Here is your bag, Samuel," Mama said. She offered him a cheek but held it distant from his kiss. The Putnams coughed and stared at their blankets.

"Keep a vigil for the boy. If he wakes that's only good. Give Nora a turn as well."

"I will watch him," Mama said. "Nora, give Father the food."

I offered the pack to Father. He took the strings in the same hand as his bag and flung both over a shoulder. I bent forward and kissed him on his rough cheek. "Do take care, Father," I whispered.

"I will, Puddin', and you do likewise,'" he whispered back. "Now farewell all and expect me back early. You, Nora, tend to Mercy before much longer, and keep an eye on . . . the barn."

I knew what he meant. I was certain now that

Mama didn't know. "Yes, Father, I will," I promised.

"We will all be busy enough, needn't worry about that," Mama finished. She pushed Father out through the door. He was still staring back into our warm kitchen when Mama pushed the door to in his face and disappeared upstairs to Zenas.

SEVENTEEN

I missed Father again, already. I missed Mama too, especially now that she spent all of her time upstairs with Zenas, talking in that hushed voice she never used for me, not for a long time gone. Since Owen. Owen—harder now to miss him, harder to remember him the way that Mama did, so strong. Mostly I missed the things we did together, the times we had, him and me and Mama all together. . . .

Time was we'd brew a tea from rose hips come the frost. For Christmas we would make the bayberry candles. In spring, before the dandelions bloomed, we'd go out greening and boil down the tender greens with pork and vinegar soon as we got home. Same way, we would find a stand of pine tall as masts and there, in cool shadow, pick the fiddleheads before they unrolled into spiny ferns. July brought raspberries. Mama dressed in Father's boots and jacket. We went all the way to Mullen's Head and back. Scratched and bitten, we would tramp home late, stained red to the elbows. Half or more we'd gobble while walking home, bugs and all. Then Mama sent us to bed while she boiled them down to thicken with sugar. The house filled with their sweetness, and so did our dreams. Morning brought cobbler thick as a plank, but soft and warm and doused with cream. In August the blackberries came, and later the blueberries. We climbed Ames' Knob raking berries up and down both sides. There were pies for breakfast, pies for supper, pies for Father coming home. And then it stopped.

Now it was only making fish and other necessaries. Mama spun, as needed, and fashioned me clothes as I grew. She helped me in the cabbage yard, growing what we could. The flower plot grew weed choked and the hollyhocks by the door rose leggy and hardly bloomed. For weeks she barely went outside, save to put the laundry out. Her churchgoing had stopped then, and without her neither I nor Father thought it proper to attend. She turned against the island people after Owen too, and talked, when she did, of being from "away." She blamed the island for what happened to Owen. I could see her ready now to do the same with Zenas Banks.

But worst of all was the waiting. Counting days till Father would be home. Counting them again till he would sail. Counting weeks till winter froze him in, then counting till the spring, the thaw, the breaking ice, when he would sail once more.

It was a common plague of counting. Already I was counting hours until Father's return from Camden. Ten hours, twelve hours, wind and tides and clearing Spindle Rock and rousing Dr. Pickering, twelve hours, fourteen. I must keep my head.

I circled the kitchen and helped Miss Batchelder. The Putnams excused themselves and retired to Mama and Father's room. I set aside the bowl of cabbage, then scrubbed the table hard, while Miss Batchelder cleared the food. The apples sat uneaten minus one. I banked the fire for the night. Already it was coming dark outside. I aired the bedclothes and fixed the palettes on the floor. But then I remembered I would be the only sleeper by the hearth this night.

At last Miss Batchelder sat in Mama's chair. She rocked it slowly, humming to herself a gentle air I didn't recognize. I tried to harmonize but just as soon the tune changed and the verse came around. Miss Batchelder didn't notice. I watched out across the Thorofare, how dark it grew. The spruces had dissolved into the night. It was still, a freezing night. The pane beside my cheek was frosting in a zigzag tracery. I pressed against it. A circle bloomed there, a porthole in the frost to see through, but nothing now to see.

Mercy. I had forgotten Mercy. I rushed to the barn and pulled at the door. It opened a handsbreadth and out skittered the cats around my ankles. The barn was dark, blacker than the night outside. I returned to the house and fetched a lantern. I edged sidewise through the door and ran full into Burgess. He lifted his head, his nose curled back in salute.

"Burgess, how are you?" I asked. He filled the barn. I squeezed around him to the stalls in back. Hay covered the floor like a tangled nest. Burgess had been helping himself. "Steady, boy," I soothed him as I reached his flanks. He rocked his head in agreement.

I reached Mercy in her stall. She blinked her brown eyes against my lantern's light. I set the lantern on a railing, then slid the stool beneath her and set the pail below. I milked her full into the pail and put it aside.

Then I climbed the ladder to the loft. I moved four bales to the edge and pushed them down. They crashed at Mercy's feet. Next was Burgess' turn. I squeezed along the loft ridge to the other end.

"Here's for you, Burgess," I called. I pushed four bales through the loft hole. They caught Burgess atop the head and rolled down. Burgess blared his rolling trumpet sound. He set to poking at the bales with his nose. Haydust flew in clouds through the loft. It sailed up my nose, and I loosed a most glorious sneeze. "Ahhhhchoooooo," I went, falling backward into the hay.

"Ruh-chhoooo," came another sneeze, from the hay at my feet. It stirred; the hay rose up and sneezed again. "Ruhhh-choooo!" This time the sneeze shook loose the hay. A face, feathered with hay but remarkably familiar, loomed out at me in the dim loft.

"Giles, it's you! Whatever are you doing in our loft?"

Giles opened his mouth to answer, but his nose spoke first, roaring out in a burst of sneezes. "I'm here to . . ." he began, then pulled his sleeve across his nose.

Hay from his sleeve stuck fast to his cheeks. "I'm here to watch over Burgess, for you as well as me, of course."

"Of course," I echoed. "To watch your precious half share, before I hide it under my bed."

"Now, Nora, you know that isn't it. 'S them Cooper boys, the others. You saw how they poked and pulled and worried over Burgess. Full of deviltry, those lads. I thought it best to keep a watch is all."

"He looks grateful for our hay, sure," I said. Below us Burgess nudged the bales end over end, stirring them up with his nose. Then he curled a sheaf into the tip of his nose and tucked it gentle into his mouth.

"And water, till I thought your well would dry. Some twenty or more buckets just to keep the trough brimful. But a wonder to watch him drink it all."

"His thirst is too great for our wee island, I'm afraid. And he'll eat five times Mercy's share, or ten or more." Well. Giles shot up onto his elbows at that, his eyes shining. Hay poked from his hair, behind his ears.

"Are you giving us notice, girl, telling us to go?" Giles snapped. He stood and found his hat buried in the hay.

"Go easy, Giles," I tried soothing him. "I just mean where's your hay, your water, your barn? I don't think Father, nor no one here, can offer enough to keep so large a creature through the winter months. Be sensible!"

"Sensible! That from a slip of an island girl that

milks after sundown!" Already, Giles was two rungs down the ladder and raging. The ladder rattled against the loft beam. Giles jumped from the third rung up and stamped around Burgess' flanks. I came down after him. He had found a trace rope fastened to Burgess' harness and tugged away. Burgess refused to lift his head from the hay. Giles found a hayrake and came around the other side. He cracked Burgess across the flanks so hard, I heard the handle split.

"Let's go, feller, come up!" Giles shrieked in the darkening barn. Again he cracked Burgess with the handle of the rake. And Burgess paid him heed this time. A mighty great dose of heed, at that, for Burgess finally lifted his head. He rolled it side to side, then lifted, reared slowly off the barn floor like a wild young colt. His two great treetrunk forelegs pawed up into the air and his giant head tilted back. His nose curled back over his head until at last, as though a spirit conjured from the empty dismal loft had arrived, that ringing melancholy bleat filled the barn, "Waaaannnnnnhhhhh . . ." It rattled off the weathered loose-nailed planks until finally Burgess dropped those legs to the ground once more. And the majesty of his size and his rearing up and the hollow echo of his soaring bleat filled the barn with the memory of something grand and divine the way a hush fills meetinghouse early Sunday.

Giles pushed the barn doors open wide and walked out into the night, leading Burgess like a young pup on his rope. "No use in following," Giles hollered back at me, "we're going up island now. You stay behind with your frail ladies and your wee boy and your old brown cow, and me and Burgess'll be fine away from here."

Behind me Mercy lowed at the insult. I shut the barn doors and ran after Giles. Burgess snorted and seemed to moan at the prospect of a march to nowhere. Giles tugged at the rope. I caught the rope and pulled it taut. Giles snapped it from my hands. Burgess halted where he stood. I lunged at Giles and caught his sleeve.

"Come back to the barn. I didn't mean that foolishness. Of course you're sensible. I was worrying about Burgess. The matter is difficult, his feeding for how long, his shelter in that cramped barn. And enough hay to feed ten teams of oxen for a week." I was pulling at Giles' sleeve, pulling him back toward home. Threads from his tattered jacket came off in my hands.

"Sensible," Giles huffed in the darkness, but I felt his arm easing under my grasp.

"Of course you are, dear sensible Giles. But we must provide for the elephant, and it will take considerable lots of food, and water."

"I will provide for him," Giles vowed, handing me the end of rope. "I will provide for him with your help and the Lord's."

"I was thinking more like getting Father and the

others, maybe all of us. I'm sure we can spare some cabbages, and others might do likewise."

"That's brilliant, girl." Giles brightened. "We will trade parts of shares for food. Say a hundredth share for a hogshead of apples, two hundredths for a peck of cabbages, a tenth for a loft of hay . . . "

"Island folks unlikely are going to want a share in Burgess, Giles," I cautioned. Giles seemed to think all humankind might share his enthusiasms. I felt not so sure. "They would do it for you, Giles, not for a share of Burgess, despite he's a marvel. They would do it for you."

"Not hardly, dear," Giles muttered. We had arrived at the barn. Giles pushed the doors open, and we led Burgess in and turned him around. "But they will for you. That's right, for Nora Beverage they will pledge the heavens and all below." Giles did his dance, skipped and twirled his way around the elephant's legs. "We will start tomorrow, from door to door, from porch to stoop, we will soften their hard island hearts and empty their cellars and their lofts."

"Just possibly," I said. Giles continued his dance. He brushed past Mercy's stall. She shifted and lowed her disapproval. Giles fetched a burr comb off a nail and fussed at Burgess' tail.

"Poor lank thing," Giles clucked as he ran the comb through the frayed and wispy tuft. "There, some better," he crowed. He held the wisp out straight and let it drop. It was hard to admire such a tail, but Giles found a way. He returned the comb to its nail and circled round in front. He shrank a hand inside his sleeve, spat on the cuff, and commenced to polishing on Burgess' leather harness. When he couldn't reach up top to finish the job, he leaned the loft ladder against the elephant's flanks and carried on. The harness cap looked none the better for all that effort.

"He's near ready for a grand fine Sunday parade, I warrant," Giles boasted.

"Assuredly," I allowed. Giles seemed pleased. He returned the ladder to the loft and hurried up its rungs. "I doubt the world has seen a finer beast," Giles declared from above. He hung his legs over the edge and sat to admire Burgess. The elephant seemed to have thoughts elsewhere. He stared straight ahead into the blank doors. He exhaled through his nose in wheezy puffs.

Giles pushed back from the loft hole and started arranging a nest. I climbed the ladder up and stood on the third rung from the top.

"I will keep a watch on him tonight," Giles offered. "I will be here if he needs me."

"You will freeze, old Giles. And you will itch, come morning," I told him. He burrowed deeper beneath the hay, spun sideways in his hay cocoon.

"I have slept in worse," he answered. "I have slept in baskets, brambles, board slat bunks, on cold stone floors. I can sleep in hay."

"But not tonight," I said. "Tonight you will sleep in

the house. There is a fire in our hearth. There is a place for me and Father there. But Father is gone to Camden for a doctor tonight. Mama is upstairs with the boy. The ladies have the other beds."

"Burgess . . ." Giles began.

"Burgess is content," I told him. "For now."'

"And your mother . . ."

"She won't know. She has scarcely left the boy for a minute. And soon he will know of his mother. The hard thing will be telling him. He has asked for her already."

Giles fell silent and sat up in the gloomy loft. He pulled hay from his face. "The harder part will be the hearing of it. That will stick with him for always. The telling will go quick." He stood, and hay spilled from his clothes.

I descended the ladder and Giles followed. We pushed loose hay into a pile in front of Burgess. Giles found another rope and looped it around his forelegs and tied it to the beam post. "This will bind him fast," Giles announced.

"You might ought tie it to your wrist," I teased. Giles seemed solemn bent to keep his prize secured.

Burgess stood stock-still. He ignored the hay, he ignored the insult of the rope. He stared empty and unblinking. His huge head seemed to be dropping by degrees, tilting downward just so slightly. The weight of it, considerable, must become a lifetime's strain.

Giles chucked him under the chin and stroked his

long creased nose. "Be a good lad. I'll see you in the morning, gentle fellow." I touched him on the leg. I ran a hand under the rope to see there was no chafing. There wasn't. "Good night, Burgess," I said. Giles pushed through the barn doors and I followed. We closed them behind us and made for the house and for sleep.

EIGHTEEN

Inside, the fire cracked and seethed. We untwisted the bedclothes on the floor and arranged them end to end. Giles lay down and studied the room, silent and uneasy. His stare fixed on Mama's empty rocker. In another minute he had risen to lay his coat across its spidery arms. He turned it around, to face backward, staring off into the dark corner beyond the pantry. Satisfied, he lay again and wrapped himself in the bedclothes. He scratched at his whiskers, sighed mightily, then tucked his head beneath the blankets and slept.

I snuffed out the lamp and did likewise. But my mind grew troublesome and sleep came fitful. I listened while the house cracked and shivered in the cold. I started once when a distant rending of wood and timber seemed to fill my head with noise. I sat to listen harder and all sound stopped.

Giles lay still asleep. The fireplace glowed, blue and orange, kettle, trivet, poker shadowed only softly now like smudges. I hugged my knees and watched the window for a speck of dawn. The window was black and empty. My legs turned gooseflesh, and I rubbed to warm them some. They felt chalky and cold. My toes grew numb. I turned them toward the fire and wrapped them with the blanket, twice around. I lay again and imagined I was sleeping.

From my room upstairs came the murmur of voices. I lifted my head to listen and discovered myself now back to back with Giles. I nudged him gently along the spine.

"They're awake," I whispered.

"Awake?" Giles sat and stared at the ceiling. Mama's voice droned now soothing, now urgent. The boy's voice came louder with each word, rising at the end with a question. "I had better get," Giles announced. Hips lurching in stiff uneven steps, he walked to Mama's rocker. He pulled his coat from the arms with a flourish and set the rocker in motion. Giles shuddered. He turned away from the empty rocking chair and stretched into his coat.

"I am not your good sweet boy, and won't be, missus," came Zenas' voice down the stairs.

"Zenas, dear boy, you must stay put." Mama tried to reason with him.

"Not your dear boy, neither, Mrs. Beverage!" Zenas shouted. A fair commotion followed, chair legs scraping, footsteps above, things being thrown.

"I should go to him," I told Giles.

"At your peril, miss," Giles said, turning toward the door.

A great thumping beat against the floor above, and then again. Something banged and rattled down the stairs and crashed against the landing wall—my chamber pot! Behind it came the thumping down the stairs. Zenas, on his one good leg, hopping down, step by step, thundering hollow against the boards. He clutched the banister for dear life and scudded over the broken porcelain scattered on the landing. His burned leg hung shining and red, bare to the hip where Father had cut his trousers.

"Zenas Banks, you are not to leave this room," Mama commanded, gliding down the stairs after Zenas. She froze there, halfway down, and looked first at me—"Nora, catch him for me, Nora"—and then across the room to where Giles stood by the door—"Giles Wooster in my house, oh never such a day again!"

"Not likely," Giles answered.

I came near to Zenas and he fell stiff and sobbing into my arms. "Now Zenas, go gentle. Mind your leg," I cautioned, propping his weight against me like a falling tree.

"Damn my leg, damn it," he moaned. And then, "It hurts, Nora, it really does hurt fierce."

"Be still," I told him. He sat on the stairs, his bad leg resting stiff across the treads.

Zenas rubbed at the tears on his face. He looked across the room at Giles. "Who is that old man?" he asked.

Giles lifted his hat from his head and then replaced it. "I am called Giles Wooster. And if it please the young man, I'll take my leave."

Giles stood in the doorway, framed by the pale

light of morning, at last. He tested the weather, exhaling slow and upward. A puff of frosty breath blossomed and rose from his lips. "Cold and colder," he said, and closed the door behind him.

Zenas looked back up at me. His round pie face was high with color. His eyes were swollen red and wet.

"Keep her away from me, Nora," Zenas pleaded. "She is telling me lies about my mother. I will not hear them more, will not, will not."

Mama walked toward us. "Zenas, I am so sorry, you are so young, like Owen was, and just as contrary. Please understand."

She lifted her hands out to Zenas, coming close. "Your mother cannot . . . be with you now . . . or ever again, I am afraid. You will see her again in heaven, I am sure."

"Will not, will not, will not," Zenas said.

"You try, Nora," Mama urged.

"Will not, will not, will not," Zenas chanted.

"It is the Lord's way," Mama said.

"Will not, will not, will not!" Zenas roared.

His fingers dug at my ribs. I held him face to face. "You will wake up the dragons in all the caves of China," I whispered. Then I kissed him on both cheeks. He pulled back and rubbed his knuckles against his eyes.

"Not," he whispered back, and squeezed his red eyes closed.

We held tight to one another. The boy's chest

heaved with breath and misery. I watched across to Mama. She stood tugging at her gown, herself near tears and beyond. I wanted then to hug her too. Behind her the bedroom door swung open. Miss Batchelder stood dazed and bleary. She arranged her face into a smile. "All up already, are we? Seems a fine grand morning coming on," she chirped.

Mama turned and nodded. "Yes, well, fine . . ." she managed barely. Behind Miss Batchelder the two sisters floated like morning ghosts.

Zenas lowered his head against my neck and rubbed his eyes into the hollow trough along my shoulder blade.

"Oh dear, the boy," Miss Batchelder let slip.

"The boy, it's the young boy," the sisters chorused to each other.

"Help him up the stairs when he is ready, Nora," Mama said. "There will be breakfast to make"—she gestured broadly in the brightening room—"and all the rest." Her voice was hollow, a surrender.

As her hand dropped to her side, the front door burst open and slammed full against the wall. Giles tripped into the house and retreated to the threshold.

"He's gone," he said. "We have lost him. I should have stayed with him. Now this and"—Giles pointed through the doorway—"you had best come take a look."

I took Zenas' arm around my shoulder and we walked, three-legged, to the door. Mama followed, and the others, shyly, lagged behind.

Together we looked out upon a frosted patch of ground leading up the swell of earth beyond the well-house and farther up to where the barn had stood. Had! For now it remained only as a pile of rough planks, broken timbers, and those few proud upright posts, all twisted into a heap of rough gray wood like a giant's game of jackstraws. There in the middle of this gray heap, up to her withers in cracked dried wood, stood Mercy. A bouquet of straw ground deliciously in her sweet stupid maw.

"It—must have—been—a storm," Mama said, stricken, half unbelieving.

"Was a storm called Burgess," Giles offered.

"Must have broke loose in the night?" I wondered.

Giles shook his head. "Didn't break loose is the problem," Giles answered. "My double hitch knot doesn't slip nor break. That's why the barn is"—Giles glanced quick at Mama and then finished—"how it is." He took a notion to wander, and pulled the barn down with him.

"Who broke loose? Who is this Burgess, will someone please explain, and right now," Mama demanded. She took Zenas by the hand and pulled him from the door, and he hopped behind on his one good leg. Next she gathered me by the hand and steered us both toward her rocker.

"The elephant, Mrs. Beverage," Giles sighed. "He was on the *Royal Tar* and stranded on a ledge when we found him . . ."

"Rajapur! Rajapur!" Zenas blurted. "So you found him."

"Burgess," Giles corrected. "Yes, we found him, me and the girl, and brought him ashore."

"I saw him first," I added. "He is half mine. He is the secret I promised you, Zenas."

"No big secret. I saw him before either of you, saw him back in St. John," Zenas boasted.

Mama sank to her rocker and let both our hands slip. "An elephant, now what else could it be? An elephant, oh certainly, never in a hundred lifetimes . . ."

"And now we lost him." Giles waved an arm toward the empty doorway, the flattened barn. "I'm going off to find him before—" He broke off his thought and turned to the door.

"I will come with you," I announced.

"And me, take me too," Zenas crowed.

Together we stood in the doorway, shoulder to shoulder. Giles disappeared around the corner of the house. Mama rose from her rocker and came at us, setting her jaw for a fight.

"I am going to find Rajapur," Zenas insisted. I pulled a coat from the hook by the door. Mama kept straight at us. I wrapped the coat across Zenas' shoulders. Mama set to shaking her head.

"You need to go upstairs," Mama said. "You need to care for that leg. It'll never heal running this way and that across the island."

"I am going to find Rajapur," Zenas repeated. He

buttoned tight the coat and pressed hard into the doorway.

Behind us Giles returned pushing a wheelbarrow, the one we had used to stack the cod. He set the barrow down and plucked Zenas from the doorway. "Come here, boy, we *will* take you in this." He lifted Zenas in both arms. I took a blanket from the floor and spread it over a nest of straw he had arranged on top. Giles set him down gently. "See how that feels, son."

Zenas squirmed and settled back. He let his burned leg stick off straight over the front edge and threw his head back into the straw. He pronounced it satisfactory.

"I will not allow it," Mama said. "I will not allow this boy to go off after some creature from halfway around the world. His leg needs care, he needs the attention of a woman—a mother, especially—now that he is . . . alone in this world."

"I will not listen to her more," Zenas protested. "She talks about my mother and doesn't even know her. She can't know about my mother. She can't."

"I understand that, boy," Giles agreed, and spun the wheelbarrow around toward the barn. Mama started marching directly for the door. I held fast in the portal. Suddenly Miss Batchelder bolted from her room and past me, out the door. She was carrying a comforter. She bent over and wrapped Zenas' leg and rested it back down on the straw.

When Mama arrived at the door, I planted myself steadfast in the doorway.

"You will have to move," Mama ordered.

I stayed put.

"Let me pass," Mama tried again.

I clamped the door frame tight with both hands. I had never defied Mama before. But somehow I knew that if there was ever a time, this was it.

I arranged myself stiffly, stern-faced in the doorway. Mama sensed my fierceness, something like her own. She rested a hand on my head and lowered her voice. "Nora, you'd best get to your room now. Your own room with a proper bed."

"No, Mama, I am going with them to find the elephant. I am sorry, but I must go. I will bring them back when I can. But for now, I want to go with them."

"I see," Mama said. She retreated into the kitchen. She went to her chair but never sat. The Putnam sisters disappeared into their room and shut the door. Miss Batchelder watched us from the doorway while I slipped out into the cold morning to follow after Giles and Zenas and the complaining, groaning, single wheel that bore his weight.

NINETEEN

Burgess must have pulled half the barn behind him. The road seemed new-leveled, the grass matted and flat as mown. Even the wheel tracks and ruts seemed flattened smooth. Along the road on either side, bushes and trees lay broken fresh, tilting back from the road or leaning together from snapped trunks.

Giles pushed the barrow, seeking out the smoothest way. Still the wheel chirped and squealed under the boy's weight. Zenas lay back, face to the sky and eyes pressed shut tight, matching the wheel squeak for squeak at every bump or gully. I walked alongside, keeping the comforter across his leg. The wheelbarrow pitched side to side as its wheel caught a rut. Giles faltered but held firm to the handles. I kept pace, ready to catch the boy should he be spilled over the side.

Slow and clumsy, we made our way to where the road split in two. The outer road led up island by tracing the eastern shore. The middle road led into the heart of the island, all forest land and sheep meadow cut in the middle by the long, dark shape of Blackwater Pond. There, as we paused, Zenas bolted up in the wheelbarrow and sniffed the air. "I smell him," he said, "down that way, follow there." He pointed down the middle road and fell back into the straw. Giles looked at me and rested the wheelbarrow while he shook his tired arms at his sides. We studied the middle road and saw the mashed brown weeds and the gouges torn in the wheel ruts.

"The boy says there, Nora," Giles exhaled. "So there it is. Can you smell him too?"

"Can't smell much past you and the boy," I told him. It was true, but Giles took my meaning wrong and growled something in his throat.

Giles took the wheelbarrow up once again and pushed on. Zenas lifted up onto his elbows now that we might be getting close. I walked ahead in lead, hoping for first sight. Soon we were winding down the long slope through Binghams' wood. As the woods thinned, the road widened and ended, spilling out into wide meadows where sheep found pasture in the spring before returning to their summer folds. Below the meadow, Blackwater Pond shone dark and flat, a great wet slate dropped from out of the sky.

"Hold tight, boy," Giles called out to Zenas. "We're out of road and into choppy water." Giles veered off right, following the long brown scar where Burgess had dragged his timbers behind. The grass seemed shorn, scraped bare in places down to wet mud, wetter as we neared the pond. The wheelbarrow bumped and rattled, rattled and whined, and Zenas bit back the pain. I slowed some and caught Zenas' sore leg, clamped onto his heel, and cradled it in my left hand to spare him the bumping.

At pond's edge we stopped, confounded to be sure. For the scar and the scraping on the earth seemed to stop at water's edge. As though Burgess must have marched right in and disappeared.

"Out there or grown wings and taken flight," Giles muttered. We stared at the pond, the dark water silent and slick.

"I still smell him, I tell you," Zenas protested. "Try over here."

He pointed along the pond's edge, and we took his lead and pushed farther along. The wheelbarrow resisted, its wheel now sinking into the soft muck beside the pond. Giles puffed mightily with the effort. Soon we had reached a stand of trees, cedar and birch growing in a tight bunch at the edge of a fen, almost a cove. Some twenty yards out in the water, as we came around the curving bank, we saw a plank, rough hewn but finely squared, floating just offshore. A timber, yes, perhaps a beam post. And snugged tightly to it, wrapping its girth twice and knotted the size of a child's fist, a rope sloped sagging from the beam and disappeared beneath the water back toward shore.

TWENTY

We pushed forward through the stand of trees and found him, lying on his side, at the edge of the cove. His backside lay just off shore, his head and forelegs settled into four feet of water or more. The rope still wrapped his legs and neck like a harness. Branches and brown leaves had caught beneath the rope and garlanded him in autumn colors. His ear fell back from his face and hung like a fallen sail just above the water's surface. That long creased nose curled into the dark pond. One open eye stared upward but saw nothing. Burgess was dead.

Giles let drop the wheelbarrow's handles and stomped knee-deep through the water up to Burgess. He tugged at his ear, looked sidelong into the one dull eye. Finally, he fell full out across Burgess' neck, laid his head flat against the animal, and wept.

I turned back to Zenas. He lay back in the tilted wheelbarrow, clutching handfuls of straw and rubbing them against his face. His cheeks had turned red and scratchy.

"It's so sad, Zenas," I said. "Poor thing weren't meant to be here, in a barn, on this island. Nor floating on a steamboat, neither."

"Too far from India, girl," Zenas added, and then burst into tears. He cried and bawled until his face shone with the tears and the rubbing of straw.

I bent toward him and raked the straw over the sides with my fingers. I tried smoothing his face, wiping at the straw and tears. He pulled his face away and twisted sideways in the barrow. This crying was no longer just for Burgess or Rajapur or all the elephants under heaven. It was something much bigger. I knew enough to let him be.

I turned to stare back up at the meadow behind me. A family of deer appeared from the trees and grazed on the brown stubble. The yearling and a six-point buck bent their necks to the ground while the doe kept watch. She twitched her head to and fro, then stood sideways against the rising gray light of morning. Behind her, in the same gray light, came a silhouette marching over the rise. The figure wore a dress and walked headlong into the deer. Startled, they disappeared into the woods, but still she came marching, dress, boots and bonnet, both arms stuffed with bundles, making a beeline right for me.

"Nora Beverage," she called, and then I recognized Mama. "Nora Beverage, did you save your blessed elephant?" She halted, finally, beside me and pushed a crock of milk, half empty, into my ribs.

"We found him, Mama, but no, we didn't save him." I pointed toward the cove, toward Burgess and Giles on top.

"Well, it's a pity and I'm sorry. For you and for Giles Wooster. Now drink some milk and thanks to God poor Mercy still's alive."

I drank deeply of the milk. The cream, clotted from the long walk up island under Mama's arm, half caught in my throat. I took another swallow and held the crock toward Mama. "The boy needs some as well, I'd venture." I nodded in the direction of Zenas, who had lifted his head from the barrow.

Mama took the crock and I followed her to Zenas. "Good morning, lad," she greeted him. She thrust the crock into his hands and told him to drink. From beneath her other arm she loosed a bundle wrapped in linen. It fell into his lap, unrolling a dozen biscuits between his legs. He stuffed one in his mouth without the first chew, then swallowed some milk and let the biscuit dissolve in his mouth. He turned his red face toward Mama.

"Thank you, mum," he said.

"Thanks nothin'," Mama answered. "Runnin' off with this wild girl and that old man to hunt after elephants. And you with that leg."

"He is dead," Zenas said. "Rajapur is dead."

"Let us pay our respects, Zenas," Mama said. "You and me and the wild girl here." Then Mama reached an arm across my back, hand against my shoulder viselike, and squeezed, gathering me into her chest until, smothered in the folds of her dress, I had to pull away to breathe.

Mama wiped at her eyes with the faded sleeves of her dress. She gathered herself and pulled at the wheelbarrow's handles until Zenas rolled forward through the damp earth. I followed, carrying the near-empty crock.

We found Giles, still clamped across Burgess, his face still buried against the creature's neck. Mama stared for a full minute at the capsized elephant. "A wonder, this will be a lifetime's wonder, Nora. Always remember."

"I will always," I answered.

"Come get some breakfast, scoundrel," Mama called. There was teasing in her voice, more now than anger. "Come, Giles Wooster, come claim your daily bread."

Reluctantly, Giles slid down from Burgess and came sloshing through the bog. "My appetite is lacking, missus, thank you please," he said with the slightest bow.

"Lacking or not, you had best eat or we'll have to bury you with your wrinkled companion," Mama answered.

TWENTY-ONE

Zenas offered a biscuit from beneath him in the wheelbarrow. I held out the milk. Giles took and ate and drank. "Was a good breakfast, Mrs. Beverage," he said, then swallowed hard and stared back at Burgess. "Now I must take care of the pitiful remains." Stooped and stiff, Giles picked a path back toward the bog.

"I say we bury him," Zenas piped up. "Dig a great huge hole up there"—he pointed back toward the meadow—"and get him down inside it. Roll a great boulder here and fashion a headstone of fine Roman letters saying:

HERE LIES RAJAPUR,
HIS JOURNEY ENDED,
MOURNED BY US,
HIS EARTHLY KINDRED.

"It would be brilliant, I tell you, brilliant and handsome and—and—gloriously monumental." In his excitement he beat at the sides of his wheelbarrow and bounced so violent that the barrow pitched sidewise. Zenas nearly spilled over, clutching at both sides to hold fast.

Mama rushed to him. I dropped the crock and

knelt beside her. She arranged the comforter and set his leg gently down. Zenas looked up at me and smiled. "Tell her you like it, Nora. Tell her how brilliant it is."

"Maybe it is brilliant," I admitted, "but it will take hundreds of shovels and years of digging, and then—"

"Not his to decide. He is mine and will remain mine and so I will decide." We turned to see Giles behind us once again. He wasn't threatening but he was dead serious. And he had forgotten something else.

"Is yours and mine, remember?" I asked, just as firm. "I saw him first and half a share is mine. Remember, you pledged it, you said it, a fifty share. That means I decide *with you*, Giles Wooster."

Giles made no answer. I sprang up and walked halfway toward him. He straightened to his full height. He raised a fist to his mouth and bit something, a slice of thumbnail, and chewed slowly, in no hurry to answer.

Mama picked up the crock by its lip and held it clenched like she might swing it at somebody. She came between Giles and me.

"No matter who decides," she said. "It's no matter for the animal least of all. No one owns him, first. You hardly owned him when he lived and that didn't go very far. Now that he's dead, he belongs to nobody. We failed him when he lived, the circus did, the people on the *Royal Tar*, the land he came from, wherever that was—"

"India, mum," Zenas piped up. "Father says they're from India, same as dragons live in China."

Mama stared out over our heads, across the flat dark surface of Blackwater Pond. She could have been looking toward India, or even China. But very far away. And when she spoke, her words sifted through the air quiet as snow. "Well, it doesn't matter where he is from. What matters is that he is here with us, at the end. Now we must honor him as best we can and let him go. Any claim you have on him comes finally to nothing more than that. For all of you. All of us. Do you understand?"

I nodded yes, and Giles stood fixed, head bent downward. But Mama seemed not to notice us. Instead she turned to see Zenas, the comforter pulled half across his face. He was crying, he was smiling, it was terrible. Mama stooped and kissed the boy. Then she stood and marched up the hill with her empty crock tucked beneath an arm.

"Stay put, stay warm," she called back to us. "I will bring others back, and there will be more food. Just stay put and wait."

TWENTY-TWO

Zenas lay sideways on the wheelbarrow. He was crying—I was sure he was crying. But when he lifted his head at last, he spat straw and wiggled his toes free of the comforter. "Your Mama is full of nonsense," he said.

"No more than you or me," I answered him. "She is just trying to make us understand. About Burgess and all."

"Oh, I understand about Burgess, Nora. I understand he is dead and that he don't belong to no one."

"Nobody," I tried correcting.

"Right, certain," he agreed. "Nobody don't belong to no one."

"Well, yes, I think maybe she means that, too."

Zenas propped himself up on his elbows. He watched back to where Mama had disappeared over the rise. "Why is she so mean, Nora?"

"She wants you to get better, Zenas. Sometimes that's how she is when she—"

"No, I mean really mean. Like she told me there aren't no dragons in China. Why does she say that? I know all about dragons—"

"Have you seen one?" I asked.

"Well, no, but I seen drawings, and the wooden

ones from China that my father brings. But your mama says that's nothing but fancy. She says the only cave they live in is my head. Pure nonsense."

"Nonsense to you, maybe. But I think it isn't meanness," I told him.

I watched back to the rise. Mama was gone. Birds flew against the sky and sank downward as if pulled by strings and disappeared into the trees.

"Not meanness, Zenas Banks," I repeated. "Just saying it because she needs to hear it too."

For the next hour or more, Giles stood at the bogside, keeping a vigil over Burgess. He prowled among the trees, eyeing first one, then another. He paused by a tall straight fir, nodding his approval.

Zenas pronounced him daft. I didn't know. So we kept a watch on Giles as he stalked among trees, muttering to himself, before returning to Burgess. He paced off steps in the mud beside the dead elephant as though taking measure. Zenas spoke at last of his mother, closing his eyes to remember the smell of her hands against his face, spicy as nutmeg, cool as wax, he said. He was fondest of her during their summers in St. John, with her sisters. She would sing harmony with the aunts and together they would gossip in the kitchen while Zenas sat by the oven holding batter spoons against his tongue and waiting for the baking smells to fill the warming air.

"Ginger nuts and Abigail's brown nutcake," he

burst out, snapping his stumpy fingers with the joy of remembering.

I told him what I could of Owen. I remembered best the line fishing for flounder off Stimpson's pier and his berry-stained face swollen with bites after picking. And after his baths, more water on the floor than in the tub. But that was all; Owen was fading. I vowed to ask Mama for more. I was certain now she would share him with me.

Suddenly, from behind us, came the squeaking of wheels and a "hallooo" rolling down the meadow. We turned, and there came Lem Carver with his team pulling a wagon. Mama sat up front and Miss Batchelder and the two old sisters in back wrapped against the chill in every coat and cloth we owned. Behind them came the Cooper boys with a passel of mothers and sisters. Thayer Parker and his mother followed behind, carrying baskets, and the rough gentlemen marched behind like a troop of soldiers. Soon nearly the whole island had appeared, like a grand holiday. Old Man Staples came from his store in a wagon stuffed with crackers and pickles and a great wheel of cheddar.

Master Simon Dunleavy, not a year removed from Ireland and come to teach at our school, brought his fiddle and tuned up with jigs and reels. He played "The Widow's Lament" while Mama passed out food, her biscuits, her beans, cold but sweet, and saw that Mr. Stimpson did the same.

As everyone ate and danced and conversed, I wheeled Zenas up to Lem's wagon to greet Mama.

"You are welcome to join us up here," Mama said. Lem jumped off and lifted Zenas up. The sisters and Miss Batchelder hurried to fashion him a nest in the bottom of the wagon, and Mama supervised the transfer. I hopped up too, and soon had nestled beside Zenas in the straw. We shared the comforter while Mama handed us morsels of food.

"Would he like something, do you suppose?" Mama asked, pointing to Giles. He stood at the elephant's side, still alone amidst the growing celebration.

Zenas and I shouted for Giles over the music. Giles turned and waved. At last he trudged from the bog, mud brown to the haunches. He came sideways clear of Mama and approached the wagon.

"Giles Wooster," Mama laughed, "crusted and begrimed worse than usual. We are offering you some food. Eat with us." Mama produced a linen folded overtop of some honeyed johnnycake. Giles shrugged and refused.

"Come eat, old Giles," she urged again. Still Giles refused.

"You are generous, Mrs. Beverage," Giles said. "I will eat when I am hungry, as I usually do."

"Usually do," Lem laughed. "Your 'usually do' keeps you bony as the undertaker's wife." He gathered himself on the bench beside Mama and roared.

Giles strode the last steps to the wagon. He

straightened his back until he stood full height. He lifted his pointy chin from his chest and reared his head back in defiance. His voice rang with the volume of purpose. He said, "Ladies and gentlemen, food can wait. You may join me in this enterprise. I invite you all. I must care for this creature, this Burgess—"

"Rajapur," Zenas insisted from the bottom of the wagon.

Giles waited, head cocked against the wind. He was in no mood. "I will build him a raft. We will take him to the center of the pond and let him go. He will be there always at the bottom of the pond that has no bottom. He will rest at the bottom of Blackwater Pond. He will be here with us forever. It is all we can do."

Giles returned to the bog where Burgess lay. We sat, others stood scattered, on the meadow above, and watched. Giles waded waist deep in mud. He stood by Burgess' flanks and seemed to test the bottom, jumping and wiggling to find the solid ground beneath.

That done, Giles took control. He flew among the trees with Thayer at his side. They notched the straightest, tallest firs. Next Giles gathered the Coopers for a talk, and they left to fetch axes and wedges, saws and rope. Mama ordered Lem to drive up to the bog, and he obeyed. The others followed, until soon the island seemed encamped across the way from Burgess. Children chased and danced along the shore; Master Dunleavy fiddled. The gentlemen gathered wood and set a fire roaring. It had become a wake and a celebration. Any chance the island had to come together they would take. Music, food, good company, any company at all, were welcome parts of any occasion strong enough to beg attendance of us all. Summer was short and full of hurried work. Winter, always coming, gray and long, a solitary time. Even an elephant's funeral—especially an elephant's funeral—was a change too good for anyone to miss.

The Coopers returned, and the Browns from the boatyard with them. They laid mightily into the notched trees, and in an hour or more twelve straight, tree trunks had been dragged to the water's edge. Giles gave the command and all hands pulled the logs into the water. They stood waist-deep in the dark bog and notched, then lashed, the ends together. They pried the loose ends underneath of Burgess and slid the lashed ends in. They circled Burgess with lines, and fifteen or twenty men in unison managed to roll his muddied back across the logs. He seemed by then a giant mound of ooze set out to dry.

The gentlemen gathered the branches stripped from the logs. They heaped them on the fire and the fire grew and blazed, cracking as the sap exploded in the green limbs. Zenas had fallen asleep in the wagon bed, so I left him to stand at the fire. "Not too close, Nora dear," Mama warned, but it wasn't a scolding voice. I stood and watched the fire as the afternoon flew by. Coopers and Browns left the bog in turns, each to warm and dry some by the fire before returning to the raft. Through the fire I watched Burgess, tilted on the tipsy raft, sunken in the middle with his weight, more a great log basket, I supposed, than a sound square raft. But it held him, and it floated, for all that.

Rapt and dazed by the majesty of fire, I started when an arm encircled my shoulders. A hand squeezed against my arm. "Well, Puddin', this has become a day for remembering." It was Father, back from Camden with the doctor. I wrapped myself inside his jacket and hugged him to me. He smelled of wool and salt water.

"Yes, Father, a day for remembering and forgetting. Did you see the barn?"

"A shambles, but Mercy is fine. We will rebuild the barn before snow."

I pointed through the fire toward Giles. "Did you see Burgess? He broke free and came here, to the pond. He was dead, over there half in the water. We can't say why."

"It isn't anything we can know," Father said. "It was the fire and the water, or the weather, or just too much to endure, too far from where he belonged. Animals can die from being lonely, or gone from their homes too long. But who will ever know?"

"Can we die for that too?" I asked. Father pulled me back some from the fire. My cheeks felt warm as hearthstones.

"I imagine it is possible," Father answered. "I have seen folks spend a lifetime dying for that." He knelt behind me and watched the fire over my shoulder.

Abruptly then, he snapped me off the ground and hoisted me high onto his shoulders. From that high perch I surveyed the meadow and the pond. Father twirled to the fiddle tune, jigging and bouncing, and we spun between couples and children marching, hands held aloft, and wagons and old men chewing food. I took it all in, around and around, the fire, the meadow, the gray rising swell of earth where the sun slid low against the sky, Giles and his men in the bog, easing the raft with Burgess to its final end, slogging in mud and hollering over the music. Me, at the center of it, atop my father's shoulders, how I saw it all at once and together, making from it all a single thread, spinning from the island and the sky, from the music and the noise and the sharp sweet burning of the wood, a thread to bind up all of us and all of this. It would make someday a cloth grand enough to cover us through the gray weather of months that never end, and keep us warm.

When we reached Lem's wagon, Father dropped me like a bundle and I bounced down beside Zenas. A black-coated man with spectacles bent over him—Dr. Pickering. It seemed like a prayer meeting, with Mama, Miss Batchelder, the Putnam sisters, and even Lem kneeling down from the bench to watch and attend.

"And who are you, child? A sister, perhaps?" the doctor murmured without looking from Zenas' leg.

"My good sister, Nora," Zenas boasted like a soldier. "She's been caring for me from the start."

"She has done well," Dr. Pickering said. "The leg will heal. The skin is sloughing already. It will hurt some more, of course. Keep it moist with the salve." He produced a blue bottle and spilled some onto Zenas' leg. It smelled of trees and peppermint.

"Mama has done the caring. I have been the nuisance is all," I confessed. "I have stolen him away to here is what. Me and that old man there." I pointed across at Giles, seen through the fire cavorting on his raft like a demon. "I have given him my bed and lent him Mama. She has nursed him entire."

"Finest kind of care, a mother's care, indeed." The doctor smiled.

Mama blushed and looked across at Father. "He was given me and it wasn't a choice that I had," she said.

"We can only choose what our hearts allow," the doctor answered. He smoothed across Zenas' hair with one hand and replaced the blanket with the other. He patted the boy's good leg. "Give it two days and then walk on it," he told Zenas. "It will hurt, will be stiff. The skin will feel like it's tearing, but you must use the leg. Promise me?"

Zenas nodded. "I promise. I will walk to St. John's Bay and back again if you say."

Lem chuckled and stood by the wagon's seat. The doctor stood down. Father scooped me from the wagon bed and lifted me to his shoulders once again. The sisters and Miss Batchelder stood down too and came beside us. A commotion stirred by the pond's edge. Folks now clustered by the bogside. A clamor rose, cries rang out.

"He's off," a voice echoed.

"All clear," rose another.

"Godspeed," came a third, then followed by a chorus of farewells and taunts, and good wishes.

"Hold me higher, Father," I urged. Father set me over his shoulders and we neared the water's edge. Mama joined us. We watched the darkening pond. From behind the crowd came floating the sagging raft, pushed sideways out by two Cooper boys, one at each corner. Giles stood at one corner. He held in both hands a long smooth alder trunk, lean and straight as a rake but ten times longer. He sank it into the water and pushed his way out. A pitch torch burned at his side, wedged between two logs.

The Coopers gave the raft a final heave and then came ashore. Giles pushed his branch down and away, poling out into the pond. He lifted the pole from the water, hand over hand. Its pale bark shone in the torchlight like china. We all of us, the island, stood and watched and fell silent.

"Please, Captain Beverage, might I join you, sir?" came a small voice from below. We turned to see Zenas behind us. He stood solid, listing just slightly to port, still wrapped in the comforter.

"Here, Mother, take your girl," Father said. He handed me over to Mother. She staggered some beneath my weight but managed.

"Goodness, child, have you been eating rocks?" she puffed, locking her arms beneath me. She hadn't held me in a long, long time, and I had grown too big for holding. But I didn't say so.

"Just your biscuits, Mama," I answered. She laughed and kissed me on the neck.

Father took up Zenas. "Next stop, St. John's Bay, what, lad?" he teased. "And the doctor said two days. Now learn to mind."

Studying Giles out there on his raft, Zenas said, "It appears there won't be a grave or a headstone."

"Not that many shovels in Maine," Father answered.

"Is he going to roll that thing over the edge?" Mama asked.

"Burgess," I corrected.

"Rajapur," Zenas said.

"Not likely," Father answered. "The raft would flip entire, and Giles with it. We will watch. Must have another plan. But knowing Giles . . ."

And so we watched. Giles let slip the pole, and it floated away from the raft. The strange craft settled now some good distance from the shore, but still not quite pond center. Giles reached down and pulled the torch from between the logs. Holding it aloft, he crawled up the elephant's side. He stood, finally, atop the high gray swell of Burgess' side, like a giant on a mountain.

The torchlight fanned across the water. It was coming night. Above, the stars grew out of the gray. Beneath the torch's light Burgess' eye shone like a small dark jewel. It had seen more of the world than any of us watching, had probably seen longer too than most, save maybe for the likes of Giles. Now it had seen its last, staring skyward into the empty star-pointed gray of our darkening night. I imagine it must have wondered, like me, how this pond, this island so far and far away, this night at the end of October, had come to be its final place and time.

And then, settled on his sagging, tilting raft at pond center, Giles held the torch aloft and tugged at a pocket with his free hand. Something silver glinted in the light. A knife. Giles slid down the elephant's side and knelt close to the edge. He sawed awkwardly near the corner of his raft. The line gave way and a crosstie timber floated free. Giles cast the knife overboard. He scrambled again up the elephant's flank. Beneath the light its flesh seemed dull, muddied, and earthen. Giles sat cross-legged. He twirled the torch above his head in great circles. The pond flashed in arcs beneath the light.

Below, more timbers loosened. They separated like fingers stretching from a hand. Water lapped between. The strange craft listed sideways. Giles scrambled closer to Burgess' head, to higher ground. Another timber broke free, and then another. The raft shuddered and rocked. Giles held the torch still. Beneath its light he stared back at us, at all of us.

Most all the island stood fixed, watching from the water's edge, silent. Then, most strange, Giles slipped a hand underneath the creature's leather cap and clutched the harness lashed beneath its chin. He nodded once toward us all and smiled broadly, warmly. His torch hand stretched above his head in salute. The timbers broke and shot free from the lines binding them tight. Burgess rolled slowly sideways as the water rose above his legs and higher. Giles looped the torch once above his head and launched it out into the night. It rose like a burning star and landed halfway in to shore. Floating and sputtering in its dying light, the torch allowed a final vision of the great gray beast rolling slowly over and down. Burgess sank quietly and disappeared beneath a shudder in the water.

And Giles with him. The pond was empty and dark. Nothing stirred out there upon the water. Pure darkness, where the water and the trees across and the sky above all folded into one. Dark like the bottom of a well at midnight. And Giles now a part of it, swallowed up and gone into the vast and bottomless water of Blackwater Pond.

"Giles! Giles Wooster!" we called, first Father, then Lem, then all of us. Our voices rose across the empty pond and came back to us. We cried out his name, then stood and listened and called it out again. No answer came. Father bent to the fire, took a burning limb and hurled it far out over the pond. In its light we saw only the drifting timbers floating separate on the water. No Giles.

"He is gone," Lem said, and Father answered, "I'm afraid he is." We stood at the pond's edge and watched into the blackness. No one spoke further or needed to.

It was then the fire collapsed, burned wood crumbling in a pile of white hot ash. A storm of sparks lifted from the fire twirling and rising like a birth of new stars. We all watched skyward as they floated up and faded. And when we lowered our stares to the fire once more, there stood Master Dunleavy outlined against the glowing ember bed. He tucked his fiddle underneath his chin and pulled the bow across the strings and conjured one long sad note that rang in our heads like a funeral chime. And the note became a song, slow and sweet, an Irish dirge, pulling us all toward the fire.

Father carried Zenas. Mama took my hand and called behind to the sisters and Miss Batchelder. Lem came along and Thayer Parker and his mother, and all the Cooper boys and the Browns from the boathouse and more. Giles' gentlemen stood quiet as a meetinghouse.

Soon near the entire island stood in a circle around the fire, watching, staying warm. No one left, nor seemed to want to. Some held hands, some stood alone and listened. The dirge changed to a slow, sweet hornpipe. Humming at my side, Mama nodded her head with the music, mouthing the words to a song I couldn't recognize. She took my hand and spun me around.

"Will you remember me fondly and think something kindly?" Mama sang in a voice sweet and pure as the fiddle.

"Yes, Mama, always," I answered. "And we should remember Giles fondly and kindly as well. I will miss him."

"I think I will too," Mama said. Father joined us with Zenas. Mama took up her song again.

"What is she singing for?" I heard Zenas ask.

Father told him she was singing a song for Giles. "She is singing Giles to sleep, son. Like a lullaby. Do you know what a lullaby is, boy?"

"Yes sir, I know," Zenas answered meekly. And then Mama loosed a laugh, not loud but fresh as new-drawn water.

"But isn't he dead, sir?" Zenas continued.

"Dead, Zenas?" Father's face emptied. He looked at Mama.

"The old man, Giles. Him with the elephant out there." Zenas turned his head toward the darkness of the pond.

"He went with Burgess, yes, Zenas," I answered.

"It was a terrible, terrible accident," Mama volunteered.

"No. The *Royal Tar* was an accident," Zenas answered.

"We can't say what's an accident. Only Giles can say for sure," Mama said. She took Zenas from Father and pulled him close between us. Her eyes were wet, strands of hair damp against her cheek like the letter C.

And Mama returned to her song. When she had finished, Father lifted Zenas and carried him up the hill, toward home. "Let's get back, ladies. Mercy will want milking and the fire needs banking. There is supper to make and much more."

"And somebody needs to get to bed," Mama added. "We have all earned a good night's sleep. Now come along."

So we followed in Lem's wagon, creaking slowly up the hill. I sat behind and watched backward toward the pond. People left the fire in bunches and straggled after us. The fiddling had stopped and the fire faded into embers glowing pink and orange. Beyond that, nothing but the wind that stirred and dropped, a sudden gust that spent itself and vanished somewhere out across the quiet water.

TWENTY-THREE

The house settled over and around me, filled with sleeping people. How could they sleep? How could anyone? I wanted to rouse them up, to yell at them and scold them for sleeping, sleeping and not caring. Giles gone for the love of an elephant. And all of us asleep for the love of a comfortable bed.

Only last night I had slept beside old Giles and now he slept alone, forever, in Blackwater Pond. How rash and foolish to let himself go down. Yes, he had loved that strange sad Burgess, but he had me too, and Zenas, and even Mama, and his gentlemen friends and more. How wretched he must be to trade us all for one.

I decided to march right up the stairs and tell them all, tell Mama the loudest if she'd hear. This night was not for sleeping but for settling accounts. There would be no sleep until all could sleep the same, until I had spoken out for Burgess, Giles, and Zenas, and until Mama heard from me for all the days of pushing me away.

Yes, I was still angry at mama for holding tight to Zenas, all hers, hers like a prize won from the sea, some jewel washed up to hoard and lock away in a secret box at the bottom of her heart. With no room there for me . . .

I sat upright and opened my eyes. A woman stood over me, holding a brilliant light that shone in my face. Mama!

"Mama, I was just coming to see you. I couldn't sleep and . . ."

"I couldn't either Nora," she answered. "I am troubled. I wanted you with me."

She stood above me with the lantern hanging a foot from my eyes. When I gathered my legs to stand, I realized she had already jammed boots onto my feet.

"Nora, I could think only of you down here," she said. "Of you and the things I need to tell you."

"I was coming upstairs just this instant," I said.

"Well, no need," Mama answered. "I am here. We can talk. But first, we must go. Say nothing more, just follow," she ordered. I found myself too confused to protest. We were outside, in the still-dark night, walking halfway along the up island road. Mama had wrapped me in a scarf, my coat. She pulled me along with one hand, her other hand holding the lantern above her head and out front. Again we were chasing through the night, Mama and me, bundled against the cold with only a lantern to guide us. I knew without asking that we would find something marvelous or terrible at the end. It would be a great steamboat aflame, or a gray wrinkled creature from a distant land, or something stranger still.

"What is it, Mama? Where are you . . ." I hadn't finished my question when Mama pulled us both to an abrupt halt. We stood finally at the top of the sloping crest that descends to the edge of Blackwater Pond. Mama lowered the lantern and studied something in the night.

"I will show you something, Nora. Then we will go home for good." Again Mama led me by the hand down that slope. The lantern swung now at her side. Soon I realized that Mama was steering us directly toward the bed of ashes where the dying fire glowed orange at the pond's edge. Mama slowed as we came closer. Slowed and then stopped.

Through the glow of the ashes we could see the stooped figure of a man. He sat hunched, head down, doubled into the trembling heat that remained. I pulled back from Mama and she dropped my hand and moved forward.

"I knew you would be here," Mama spoke to the figure. Then, unfolding in a gray wet heap, the figure stood.

I had never believed in ghosts, nor had I ever any reason not to. But when that gaunt gray shade of a man rose to his feet on the other side of those ashes, I knew it was time to begin. I pulled back farther behind Mama and stared. He stood unspeaking, wrapped now, I could see, in a strange tangle of harnesses and straps. When he at last stepped toward the ashes, I could see the legend "Burgess" inscribed across his chest.

"So you couldn't leave us after all, not yet," Mama said to the figure.

"Not yet, no ma'am," he answered weakly. And

smiled so sheepish and tugged half in shame at the leather straps across his chest that I laughed out loud to see that my ghost was nothing more than Giles.

"Giles Wooster! Look at you," I called from behind Mama. "And we thought you had gone down with Burgess. We thought you were . . . well, dead."

"Dead, well, I tried, Miss Nora, but it weren't as easy as it looks," Giles answered.

Mama walked around the fire and draped her coat over Giles' shoulders. I followed and tied my scarf around his neck.

"You'd better come home with us and dry off and get warm, Giles Wooster. And then you'll explain yourself to all the island when the time is right." Mama tried to pull him by the sleeve, but he resisted.

"You'd better come along, Giles," I said. "You should have seen us. We sang you farewell, and danced you a dance. It was grand."

"Was grand, I know, I saw it all from the water." Giles explained how he had grabbed hold of the harness cap, and tossed the torch away, expecting to go down with the elephant. "But she broke loose, see?" Giles continued, holding out the ragged ends of the leather. "And when she did there was nothing to pull me down but my weight. So I grabbed ahold a timber come floating by and waited and watched you all and listened to you all yellin' for me."

"And didn't answer a peep," I scolded. "Not one single word."

"Nothing to say but I'm sorry. And that's common knowledge in these parts." Giles looked toward Mama and she turned away. She pulled at his elbow and he stumbled toward her. Once moving, she pulled him along. I seized the lantern from her and followed behind.

"The sorriest part is what you have done to Nora, running around hither and yon after that sad creature. And sleeping with him in the barn. And him wrecking a perfect timber barn with winter coming and a milk cow needing shelter, needing hay. You'll be building a new one in the morning once Captain Beverage finds you back. And you'll not go elsewhere till it's done."

Giles jerked his elbow free of Mama's grasp. "Then you mean I'm bound to the Beverages, tooth and nail? Glory! Making an indentured servant out of a sorry old salt like me?"

"Exactly. Something bothers you with that?" Mama answered.

"Not at all, missus. Fair enough for me," Giles answered.

"And you, Nora?" Mama added.

"Fair enough for me, the same," I said.

"Then it's settled," Mama declared. "Now let's get home."

By the time we got downstreet once again, the eastern sky was faint and gray, coming on to dawn. Giles had seized the lantern from me, claiming it was his duty to carry the light. He was almost running as we came near home. But when we reached the door he turned and blocked the way.

"One final thing, Mrs. Beverage," he began.

"And what's that, Giles?" Mama asked.

"I was wondering how you knew. How you knew to come looking after me when all the others figured I was gone."

"That's right, Mama, how did you?" I added.

Instead of answering, Mama took her coat from Giles' shoulders and put it on herself, buttoning each button with painful deliberation. Next she relieved him of the lantern. She lifted the chimney, blew out the wick, replaced the chimney and set the lantern beside the door. When finally her answer came, it came for me, to me, and Giles seemed half forgotten.

"I knew he was there because he was too alive to give in." She paused and started over. "No one dies from sorrow, Nora, nor should they. Maybe only in poems and old songs. Grief grows up and walks away. Like a child that crawls, then walks, then grows and leaves the home. Comes the time it has to leave and we must let it go. I knew it would happen for Giles, just as it happened for me. Do you understand that, Nora?"

"Yes, Mama, I understand," I said. For the first time in forever I felt that Mama had spoken from the heart.

"Your Mama is strange and wonderful," Giles said. "If she was my mother, I . . . I . . ."

"You what?" I prodded, pushing toward the door.

"Well, I would be as proud as a man that owned ten elephants," Giles concluded.

"Giles, friend, you had better try again," Mama laughed. She pushed around him and opened the door. "Now get inside the both of you."

"Twenty elephants, thirty elephants," I was saying when Mama cupped me gently around the neck and pulled me toward the door.

And then, together, we went inside.

EPILOGUE

They left next day with Father on the *Veto,* all of them—Zenas and Dr. Pickering and Miss Batchelder, still wearing Mama's bonnet, and the two old sisters. When Father returned days later, he brought gingham for Mama from the Boston stores, yellows and reds and blues, like the sky. Father set Giles to work and together they built a winter shed against the house for Mercy. The barn would have to wait for spring. Winter came fast and hard. Mama welcomed Bob and Spindle into the house for once and always. The wind blew and snow came down and blew away. The Thorofare froze hard and so did the bay, all the way to Camden. Some nights, cold, cold nights, we slept in front the fire, me squeezed tight between Mama and Father, listening half the night to their gentle breathing. Days Mama sewed dresses from her gingham. Her faded Boston dress became an apron and then, stuffed with straw, a bed for both the cats. The fish stew kept us warm and full, and the salt cod lasted near the way to March.

March brought warm winds and mud. By the end of March Father was out in the *Veto* once more, from Quoddy Head to Frenchman's Bay. April came warmer still and green. Mama wore her yellow dress and blossomed like a jonquil. She took me greening for dandelions before the first blooms made them bitter. We picked fiddleheads on Mullen's Head and boiled them with salt pork. Father feasted the night he returned. He said little but ate generous bowls, smiling to himself with each spoonful. Mama and I sensed something different and strange, but waited. Finally, he pushed his bowl aside. He pulled a letter from his pocket and read. It was from Captain Elijah Banks, father to our Zenas. This is what it said:

> Dear Beverages,
>
> My son Zenas has urged me daily to write you of his recovery. His leg is almost whole, if somewhat weakened. It will grow stronger with time. Zenas calls you his island family and remembers you all fondly. You have given generously and acted nobly on his behalf. Our gratitude is immeasurable and falters in expression.
>
> Once again this summer, Zenas will be visiting his uncle Eleazar in St. John's. He urges me to ask your permission to make a sojourn at your island home on his return. I do so knowing little of the hardship such a visit might impose. Still, Zenas needs to renew a deep attachment he has formed with your island. He speaks often of his "island mother" and the real mother he has lost. He speaks of course of Nora, and Captain Beverage, and the boy Owen, and of his closeness to the whole of

you. He speaks with much feeling as well of one Giles Wooster and the elephant who made with him that difficult passage on that stormy October night in the waters off your shore. His interest is such that I feel that a sojourn there might be a profit to his spirit and a boon to his continued recovery. For his part, Zenas reassures me that this visit is necessary and I need only your consent.

Please feel no urgency to respond. Just know that Zenas is well, has much to say about the kindness of the Beverages, and will always remember the autumn of the *Royal Tar*.

Yours, etc.
Capt. E. Banks

Mama found the ink and Father fetched a pen. They sat with me around the table that night as I composed, in my own hand, a response to Captain Banks. The words were my own, as well. That night I retired early knowing I would see the boy again. And so began, with much delight, the waiting, and the counting off of days.